MW00653713

The Assignment

Book One of the series
*The Adventures of
Fearless Fredd
(with Two d's)!*

Written by
Frederick G. Fedri

Illustrations by RKS Illustrations

Cover by Germancreative

Reader Reviews

Really enjoyed reading your book. Each chapter is its own story. Highly recommended! J. Cavalier

The book is a lot like the stories in *The Wonder Years* – heart-warming, humorous, and entertaining. An enjoyable read of those innocent and timeless days. C. Murray

Excellent read! The storytelling and editing style makes this book come alive with relatable vivid anecdotes. D. Hill

Both kids and adults will enjoy this book. Reminds me of stuff I did growing up! D.C.

I love the stories, and the fun part was you never know what is coming! I enjoyed it! Himan

Reading this is time well spent—a nice easy read filled with vivid memories of golden childhoods. JMS

My eight year old enjoyed this book very much. He loved the part about the rocketship, and where the shopkeeper gave the kids a nickel. I won't spoil the surprise for you! Frida M.

Anyone not from Upstate NY will get a feel for a special region of the country. Ari S.

A witty trip back to a time when life was simpler. Joe M.

Masterfully written. Warm hearted and fun to read! J.W.C.

A Really Important Notice

Information on people, places, TV shows, things, and events can be found in <u>Fredd's Fractured Glossary Of Interesting Facts</u> located at the back of the book. Look for <u>underlined text</u> in the story and scoot back there to be amazed and amused.

Like the book, it's mostly accurate, at least by Fredd's free-wheeling standards.

Fifty percent of book proceeds are donated to reading and literacy programs around the world.

PREFACE

The year was 1958. America's _Explorer 1_, took off from Cape Canaveral at 10:48 PM on January 31st, setting the stage for a winner takes all race to the moon. By an incredible stroke of cosmic good fortune, four friends, a rocket club, spelling contests, and a puppet show all converge to teach lessons on courage and the importance of trying again.

The four stories contained in this book detail Fredd's misadventures as they set the stage for the hilarious train-wreck ending in the final chapters of "Catastrophe in Mrs. Nelson's Class."

In story one, "Oh! Brother?" we learn how Fredd's wish for a baby sister goes undelivered in the middle of the night. After watching his favorite TV show, _Jet Jackson_, starring Captain Midnight, Fred decides to add an extra 'd' to his name for reasons only he can explain.

In story two, "A Gremlin in the Attic," Fredd's quest to discover details of his crash landing on Planet Earth hits a creepy roadblock. He only has circumstantial proof, but he is pretty sure there has to be evidence somewhere hidden in the house. When his parents warn him not to explore the attic, his suspicions are all but confirmed.

Story three, "The Rocket Club," details the efforts of Fredd's rocket club as it tries to help NASA get to the moon using fizzy powered rocket propulsion for starters. They are surprised when NASA closely adopts their first club insignia.

In the last story, "Catastrophe in Mrs. Nelson's Class," Fredd and his puppet show crew wonder if they will be fired by the school principal. In light of all the calamities and disasters that befall their performance, Fredd is sure she certainly would have if she could.

It all takes place at a time when phones were not mobile, car <u>curb feelers</u> were cool, television shows were all in black and white, mimeograph machines were state-of-the-art, and bookmobiles were the closest thing we had to the internet.

Based on the concept that true stories are more amusing when embellished freely, this book is sure to entertain.

License/copyright/ISBN

The Adventures of Fearless Fredd (with Two d's)!

Book One

While based on actual events, the book is a fictionalized account of stories, people, and places encountered during the author's 1950s childhood in Niagara Falls, NY.

Illustrations by RKS Illustrations

Cover design by Sara McMullin

Copyright © 2019 by Frederick Fedri

All rights reserved.

No part of this book may be used or reproduced or transmitted in any form or by any means , electronic or mechanical, including photocopying, recording or any information storage and retrieval system without written permission of the author.

Second Edition

Library of Congress Cataloging Data

Fedri, Frederick G.

The Adventures of Fearless Fredd (with Two d's)! - Book One / Frederick Fedri - 1ˢᵗ ed.

Summary: A story of how America's race to the moon, four friends, a spelling bee, and a puppet show all converge to teach a valuable lesson on failure and finding the courage to try again. Santa Claus, a fishing net, soda pop bottles, a science fiction movie, and a gremlin living in the attic get into the act, and it all happens within earshot of the Eighth Wonder of the World.

ISBN	978-1-7332209-0-3	(paperback)
ISBN	978-1-7332209-1-0	(hardcover)
ISBN	978-1-7332209-2-7	(eBook)

1. 1950s – Fiction 2. Puppets – Fiction 3. Childhood – Fiction
4. Friends – Fiction 5. Niagara Falls – Fiction
6. Rocketry – Fiction 7. School – Fiction
8. NASA – Fiction 9. Classroom – Fiction
10. Courage – Fiction 11. Santa Claus – Fiction
12. Grandparents – Fiction 13. Space race – Fiction
14. Nostalgia - Fiction

Disclaimer

Except for names given to Mom, Dad, Grandma, Grandpa, brother Ronnie, best friend Joey, Cubby (Wendy's puppet), Aunt Helen, and Mrs. Nelson, any attributes, quoted responses, actions or personality traits characterized in this book, should not be attributed nor associated to any classmate, friend or person that existed or attended Cleveland Avenue Elementary School at any time.

Dedication

Dedicated to our grandson, Beckett Frederick Thomas, with special thanks to my gifted wife, Pauline, for her enthusiastic support and insights as a reading teacher, and to our extraordinary children, Karen, Jonathan, and Melanie, their spouses Alan, Stephenie, and Nikhil and everyone who provided encouragement along the way.

Heartfelt thanks to my sixth-grade teacher, Mrs. Nelson, my Freshman English Professor, Mr. Brover, and all the teachers who taught me the importance of reading and writing. These skills have become even more essential as technology, electronic communications, and the volume of new information continues to expand.

Special Thanks To:

Ronnie Fedri
Joey Carosella
Dave Hill
Joel Kobren
Joyce Maguda
Sara McMullin
Carol Murray
Wayne Notto

Table of Contents
Story One: Oh! Brother?

Chapter One: Nightmare on Whirlpool Rapids Bridge   2
Chapter Two: Be Careful What You Wish For!   11
Chapter Three: Ronnie's Guardian Angel Gets a Medal   14
Chapter Four: The Great Piggy Bank Heist   17
Chapter Five: The Big Bang Strikes Again!   24
Chapter Six: You Could Call Me Fearless!   27

Story Two: A Gremlin in the Attic

Chapter One: Area 51   33
Chapter Two: Santa's Watching!   38
Chapter Three: Saturday Morning Test Patterns   45
Chapter Four: It's All About the Fish   52
Chapter Five: My Friend the Saint   60

Story Three: The Rocket Club

Chapter One: Friends Are Friends, No Matter Who Is Best   64
Chapter Two: If It's 1958, What Are You Doing Here?   73
Chapter Three: "3-2-1-0 Blastoff!"   78
Chapter Four: Fizzy Powered Rocket Fuel   83
Chapter Five   Mr. Maroon Saves The Day The Earth Stood Still   87

Story Four: Catastrophe in Mrs. Nelson's Class

Chapter One: Duck and Cover!   92
Chapter Two: The Assignment   100
Chapter Three: Dust-to-Dust, Do or Bust   105
Chapter Four: Let the Puppet Shows Begin!   115
Chapter Five: Team 5, You're Up!   121
Chapter Six: The Bee That Spelled Trouble with a Capital T   126
Chapter Seven: Before the Fall   132
Chapter Eight: Can the Principal Fire Us?   136
Chapter Nine: I'd Like to Play a "Do-Over" Card Please!   151
Fredd's Fractured Glossary of Interesting Facts   155

Story One
Oh! Brother?

Chapter One
Nightmare on Whirlpool Rapids Bridge

Have you ever visited an awesome place and wondered what it would be like to live there? I never had to, because I was born in the town known as the Honeymoon Capital of the World —Niagara Falls, New York.

Young couples, old couples, kids, kings, parents, and princesses come from all over the world to be wowed by what I saw every day whizzing around on my trusty Schwinn bicycle.

But, no matter who you are or how much you travel, the experience of seeing Niagara Falls for the first time is something nobody forgets. Summer, fall, winter or spring, the reaction is always the same.

First, you hear a constant sound of rolling thunder somewhere off in the distance. As you move closer, an unmistakable vibration begins to rattle through your shoes, letting you know that something gigantic and powerful is lurking nearby.

Bravely moving closer, you hear the unmistakable roar of rushing water as thousands of invisible water droplets begin to cool your face. Suddenly, your eyes open wide to drink in the panoramic view of *1 million gallons* of water per second cascading down 180-foot high cliffs to the churning emerald green river below.

It's no wonder that after all the "Ooohs!" and "Ahhhs!" most people experience an uncontrollable urge to visit a restroom—ASAP!

Folks visiting for the first time wouldn't know it, but everybody who lives in my city always refers to the American Falls, the Horseshoe Falls, and the Bridal Veil Falls as simply, "The Falls." It's like a nickname for a friend that just happens to be a world-famous celebrity—a shorthand way of saying, "Yeah. The Falls and me go way back. We're like family."

It's all pretty great, except there's this one tiny hitch. Well, actually, there's two.

For starters, all of the best views of The Falls are in Canada. To prove who was right, the United States and Canada built the Whirlpool Rapids Bridge so people could walk across and see the difference for themselves.

Second, walking across the Whirlpool Rapids Bridge is a terrorizing, nail-biting experience that can haunt your dreams for weeks. Thankfully, my bridge nightmares ended after one special trip that began when my grandpa Nono, hollered up the back hallway stairs, "Freddy! We go see Zia Delina. Subito!"

I knew that "Zia Delina" meant my Aunt Delina and "subito" meant, "Get over here now!" in my family's native language, Tyrolean, which mixes Austrian and Italian with a few words that Hannibal's soldiers shouted at their elephants while crossing the Alps on their way to sack Rome.

Standing as still as I could, Mom dressed me in my Sunday best. In quick succession, she guided my legs into a pair of perfectly pressed pants, my arms into a crisp white shirt and a beige jacket, and my feet into socks and a pair of highly polished black shoes. She finished it off with a polka dot bow tie.

Mom looked me over like a drill sergeant inspecting a new recruit. "Now remember to listen to Nono. If you are good, Aunt Delina has ice cream and apple strudel waiting for you, okay?"

With the mention of two of my most favorite treats in one sentence, my resistance to another treacherous trip across a dangerous gorge collapsed faster than the bridges in all of my nightmares.

"Okay, Mommy!" I replied. At four years old, I knew my priorities.

"Freddy!" I heard my grandpa calling up the stairs again.

"I'm coming, Nono!" I shouted as Mom finished straightening my bow tie.

As I walked down the green linoleum-covered stairs to my

4

grandparents' flat, all I could think of was Aunt Delina's bright kitchen and the treats she had prepared just for me.

Nono was ready and waiting. With his favorite pipe and a small cloth bag containing a thermos of milk and an apple, we set out through the front door and down the porch steps. Waving goodbye to my Grandma and Mom, we were off to Canada.

Nono worked hard all his life as a stonemason, making fireplaces, bridges, and buildings out of rocks dug up from nearby fields. He looked like Santa Claus with his bright twinkling eyes, a handlebar mustache, and a big laugh that made you feel good inside. I imagined that all he needed was a full beard and a red suit to win the Santa look-alike contest held each year for the annual Christmas parade.

Hand in hand, my grandpa and I walked along sidewalks shaded by leafy Dutch Elms without a care in the world. At least that's how it was until a newly painted sign next to the bridge came into view.

The sign was enormous. On it was a line drawing of a bridge over swirling water with a bunch of words written in big black letters.

Seeing the rocky gorge and hearing the whirlpool's angry water, I had a pretty good guess of what the sign said:

This is the Whirlpool Rapids Bridge. Kids Under 5 Years Old May Cross at Their Peril. The Bridge Authority Strongly Advises You to Go Home NOW While You Still Have a Chance.

I took some deep breaths. No sign was going to get between me and the delicious treats waiting across the border!

Cars choked the roadway in front of the bridge entrance as they jockeyed for a position. Undaunted, Nono and I closed the gap to the walkway for the trip across. A sign with a walking stick figure above the right side of the bridge pointed the way.

Just before stepping onto the bridge, I summoned up a new superpower I accidentally discovered while riding my tricycle in our garage. It seems that bare metal handlebars can scratch the paint off your dad's new car even if you don't want them to.

The second it happened, a fabled story about George Washington popped into my head. It seems even George's dad had to point out there was a dead cherry tree in the front yard before young George confessed to the deed. Figuring George was an American hero and all, I decided to wait and see if Dad saw the scratch, before I would do the honorable thing and fess up exactly like George did!

Still, it bothered me. I couldn't make the scratch go away, but I did discover that if I squinted my eyes just right, the scratch began to disappear. In fact, the more I squinted, the more it disappeared!

Like most superpowers, you never know when you need to use them until you have no choice. If squinting could disappear a seven-inch long scratch, why couldn't it disappear a deep 7-mile long gorge with its very own deadly whirlpool?

Squeezing my grandpa's hand tightly, and with full power

directed to my squinting eye muscles and puffed-up cheeks, I began tiptoeing my way across the bridge as softly as I could.

Halfway across, I felt something wasn't right. A moment later, I heard the "woohoo-woohoo!" whistle of a steam-powered train about to pass by. I didn't have long to guess how close it was because all of a sudden, the metal bridge supports groaned in loud protest while the wooden boards shook fiercely under my feet. "Trano!" yelled Nono while pointing to the steel deck above our heads.

Just as the train's shaking reached nine on the Richter Scale, my squinting powers gave out. Defenseless without my superpower, my eyes couldn't help but pop wide open. And boy was there a lot to see!

I had walked this entire time between my grandpa and a metal railing with spaces big enough for a kid to fall through. I could see the whole gorge without anything getting in the way. Rope bridges in Tarzan movies looked safer than this!

I quickly changed sides with Nono, but my feeling of safety lasted for only a second. Looking down to my left, I saw open spaces around each steel support girder big enough for both my grandpa and me to fall through!

"Nono!" I yelled as best I could over the rhythmic din of the train. He couldn't hear me, so I tugged on his hand like our lives depended on it. Nono looked down at me and smiled reassuringly. He pointed straight ahead and shouted, "It's okay, Freddy. Valda! Look!"

We were almost at the end of the bridge. The last rail car announced the train's exit with a final steel-on-steel squeal followed by a loud thud. "Whew!" I thought as my squinting superpower turned back on.

Nono looked down at me with a worried look on his face. "Freddy, when la guard say, 'Where hue born?' joost say, 'E-You-Knighted States.'"

Trying to decipher my grandpa's mixture of Tyrolean and broken English, I finally figured out what he wanted me to say. "Okay, Nono," I replied.

Gingerly stepping off the last few inches of the walkway, I finally took in a full breath and let it out. "We made it Nono!" I exclaimed.

I released the death grip I had on my grandpa's pinky finger and rubbed my sore eyes.

With my squinter power off, I saw a white line painted on the walkway and another sign, probably written in Canadian. I guessed you couldn't just walk into any country, no matter how friendly they were. You had to stop and say hello first.

Stepping forward, my grandpa whispered, "Ricorda.

Remember."

Without a hint of how his day was going, the border agent studied my grandpa before politely asking, "Where were you born?"

Before my grandpa could even start to open his mouth, I blurted out the answer I had practiced for the last ten minutes. "OVER THERE!" I exclaimed as I pumped my pointer finger to make the exact location crystal clear.

Caught by surprise, the agent looked down at me and, with a big grin, said, "Well then, young man, welcome to OVER HERE!"

As Nono grabbed my hand to hurry out, I remembered to say, "THANK YOU!" as loudly as I could. I figured if I were extra polite, he'd remember us for sure. Not only that but next time, he wouldn't have to ask such a silly question.

With our feet firmly on solid ground, Nono hoisted me onto his shoulders and said, "Goot job, Freddy!" My grandpa was proud of me! As we bounced along, he repeated, "Goot job! Goot job!" with each bounce.

Looking around from my new vantage point, now a good six feet off the ground, the sun was brighter, and the view of The Falls even more spectacular. We were on our way to gorge ourselves on the treats awaiting us in Aunt Delina's kitchen.

At that moment, I knew that I didn't have to be afraid anymore. In my dreams, whenever floorboards began falling, or railings began disappearing, I'd climb up on my grandpa's strong shoulders. Like a hero in an action movie, he'd always get me safely across.

At the end of my prayers that night, I said, "God bless Mommy, Daddy, Ronnie, and Nona." Then I closed my eyes and finished with a loud, "And God bless my grandpa. Amen!"

Chapter Two
Be Careful What You Wish For!

When you are four years old, you start to remember big things. Like the time Mom woke me up from a sound sleep in the middle of the night. "Frederick, Nona and Nono are waiting for you. Muoviti. Va zo!"

As I desperately tried to cling to sleep, Dad picked me up in a whoosh and whisked me downstairs to my grandparents' flat.

Before I knew it, I was seated at the kitchen table, snug in my bunny-eared pajamas and hugging my stuffed toy horse, Trigger, I watched as my parents left the house in a big hurry. Bleary-eyed and stunned, I knew something big was going on. What exactly, I had no idea.

"Freddy, what do you think? Brother or sister?"

Nona, my grandma, had just given me a choice. Not wanting to be rushed on such a critical decision, I quietly pondered the question as Nono handed me a mug of freshly brewed, caffeinated coffee, complete with milk and three spoons of sugar.

"Dreenk la café, Freddy. You feel poo behm," Nona offered in her normally soothing tone of voice. I knew "poo behm" meant "much better," but right now I was half-asleep and lucky to understand anything, English or Tyrolean.

Taking a long sip, then placing the mug back on the kitchen table, I did my best to slow down time even though the pendulum on my grandma's cuckoo clock had a different idea. As far back as I knew, none of my four-year-old friends ever got to offer their two-cents on such an important matter. What I decided, right then, would affect my entire life!

I slowly pondered the question. Outwardly I appeared calm, but my mind was spinning like a toy top. I considered all my options again. "Brother or sister? Hmm?" Looking down at the crumbs and spilled coffee on the table, the answer hit me like a ton of bricks. Grinning from ear to ear, I exclaimed in a strong and confident voice, "A sister!"

Nona laughed, "Subito, vee see."

You might ask, "Why a sister?" Well, it was simple, really. In my nearly four years of witnessing all the work my mom, aunts, and grandma did around the house, I realized that a sister was the right choice to get me out of all kinds of chores. A baby brother, on the other hand, was too big of an unknown to take a chance.

Grasping what was at stake, I blurted out, "Nono. Nona! I need to call Mommy and Daddy right NOW!"

Spinning around, I spotted the phone on the countertop behind me. Looking at the shiny contraption with its white dial face and big numbers, I realized I had no clue how to use it. My grandma calmly shrugged her shoulders and apologized,

"No numbero. No bon telephono." The message was short, but it was bad news, just the same. They didn't have the phone number, so they couldn't make the call.

Any hope of a last-minute message getting through to my parents was gone. All I could do was cross my fingers and wait. Just then, the clock made a metal scraping noise. We all turned to watch as the doors opened, and a little bird figurine appeared, announcing what it thought about my dilemma. "Cuckoo! Cuckoo!" it announced merrily.

Slumping in my chair, I realized that decision-making is nerve-racking, especially when you don't have any control and you just gobbled down half a loaf of Italian bread dunked in a mug brimming with coffee and sugar. Jittery or not, I just needed to go back to sleep and hope for the best.

Two days later, my parents finally arrived home. Peering into the bassinette, I took a deep breath, crossed my fingers, and asked my Mom, "Is this, my new sister?"

"No, it's your baby brother, Ronnie," Mom replied proudly.

"Oh! brother?" I sighed heavily.

Mom didn't waste any time, "Be a good big brother and help Daddy unload the car, please!"

"Mom?" I asked innocently. "Before you and Dad go out again, could you show me how to use the telephone? Please!"

13

Chapter Three
Ronnie's Guardian Angel Gets a Medal

In spite of the big snafu at the hospital and Ronnie's two-year struggle to learn how to speak with words I could figure out, we eventually did hit it off pretty well.

Ronnie soon learned what I already knew. Simply put, we were lucky to have a set of great parents and grandparents whose mission seemed to include lectures on how to avoid every possible unsafe thing we would ever encounter during our entire lives on this planet. None was more important than their warning to never stick a metal butter knife into an electrical outlet.

One bright morning, in a stunning example of personal sacrifice, Ronnie decided to conduct his very own knife-poking experiment to demonstrate the importance of following all the rules on electricity, especially avoiding contact with it at all costs.

I remember the exact moment like it was yesterday. Ronnie was in his chair, quietly eating breakfast as Mom busily returned a bottle of milk to the refrigerator. Shooting a sheepish grin in my direction, Ronnie dropped to the floor, butter knife in hand, and set a path straight for the closest electrical outlet.

Even with the refrigerator door blocking most of her view,

Mom's early warning system detected unusual motion and noise in the kitchen. "Red Alert! Red Alert!" Mom's head quickly appeared above the door, scanning first me and then the kitchen floor.

"Ronnie! Don't!" Mom shouted now fully at the highest military readiness status known in missile command circles as DEFCON 1.

From where I sat, positioned with a spoonful of milk-soaked Kix just inches away from my lips, I could see her warning was going to be a little too late.

Sparks flew out of the wall, as an invisible force silently propelled Ronnie backward, gliding along on a frictionless surface thanks to Mom's zillion coats of liquid floor polish. With a thin trail of blue smoke marking his trajectory, Ronnie finally skidded to a halt, stunned but safe, just inches away from Mom's feet.

More sparks shot out of the outlet before all the lights in the house flickered and went out. Ronnie's butter knife was now firmly welded to the inside of the outlet box.

Sitting on the floor, it took Ronnie only a split-second more to compose an appropriate response, "Owee Owee Owee!"

"Let Mommy see! Promise never, never do that again!"Picking my brother up in her arms, Mom hugged then scolded then hugged again.

For everything that could have happened, Ronnie had

escaped harm, needing nothing more than a diaper change.

Clearly, Ronnie's guardian angel had just earned another Distinguished Service Medal. The third medal that month for valor shown in life-saving efforts performed in the nick of time. If any angel needed a vacation, it was definitely Ronnie's.

The next day, white plastic safety covers appeared on every outlet in the house. My parents could have saved their money. I already checked off 'Electrical Outlet and Butterknife Experiment' from my to-do list.

Chapter Four
The Great Piggy Bank Heist

"Ronnie. Where's my money?"
I was lucky if my brother even
knew what the word money
meant, being he was 3 years old
and still hadn't demonstrated any
skills that would warrant him
getting any kind of an allowance.
In fact, by my calculations,
Ronnie owed Mom plenty of
dough for the tons of laundry soap she needed to wash his piles
of stinky cloth diapers.

"Clink! Clink! Piggy bant." Ronnie said, pointing to the
piggy bank on our shared nightstand. How he decided bank
ended with the letter t was beyond me.

By now, my brother was at least able to express himself
in incomplete sentences. Most of the time, I could barely
understand him, but this was an emergency. I needed to get all
the facts and get them fast.

Calling on all my natural powers of sign language
embedded in my genetic code, I frantically began gesturing like
a tourist from a foreign country who had just lost his wallet
down a sewer drain. Feverishly, I pointed at my white ceramic
piggy bank, then back to me all the while slowly speaking two
simple words: "S-h-o-w M-e." Hitting my chest on 'Me.'

It was a desperate technique I learned from Mom while

watching her attempt to figure out what Ronnie had swallowed when she wasn't looking.

Ronnie grinned. He got the message. Picking up the only coin remaining on my half of the nightstand, he positioned it over the piggy bank opening and dropped it in. "Clink" went the coin. "Clink," Ronnie repeated with a smile.

"Oh, no. You didn't." I yelled in agony.

Ronnie didn't understand. A puzzled look replaced his triumphant grin. As he eyed the bedroom door behind me for an escape route, I blocked his way and pressed on with my interrogation.

"How many clink clinks?" I demanded. "Five?" I held up my hand with five fingers wiggling inches from his nose.

Ronnie shook his head, no.

"Seven?" Adding two fingers to my right hand.

Ronnie shook his head no again.

Reaching over, Ronnie pulled up my last three fingers.

"All of them?"

My brother's proud smile told the story. The message was all too clear. Yessiree Bob. All of my allowance money: three dimes, two nickels, and five pennies were entombed in the ceramic piggy bank, now appearing all the more obnoxious with its silly spiteful grin. I had to figure a way to make an emergency withdrawal because tomorrow morning Joey and I had plans to go halfsies on a new rocket model we spotted in the window at the Ace Hobby Shop.

Taking a deep breath, I consoled myself that as far as problems go, this was a simple one. After all, it wasn't like the money was lost or anything. It was safely tucked just a few inches away inside a smiling ceramic pig's stomach.

Sitting on my bed, I considered all my options. If the money went into the slot with no trouble, it should come out just as quickly.

Holding the piggy bank upside down, I began to shake it violently. No luck. Running to the kitchen, I made a beeline for the silverware drawer. Just as I was about to pull open the drawer, Mom walked into the kitchen, catching me red-handed.

"Frederick. What are you doing?"

I gave the best elusive truthful answer that I could think of, "Uh, I need a butterknife for my allowance money?" Ending my response with a question mark sure made it sound like there was an activity somewhere that might not happen unless I got my hands on one right away.

Surprised that I might actually be doing housework without being told, Mom pleasantly advanced her interrogation, "Are you cleaning something?"

"Yes, Mom." Which was kind of the truth? After all, I was trying to clean out my piggy bank as fast as I could.

Opening the kitchen drawer, she handed me Ronnie's butterknife complete with its distinctive blue burn mark etched into its otherwise shiny metal surface.

"In that case, don't let me stop you. But be careful."

Without any clue as to what exactly was really going on, Mom had provided another safety rule as a final warning.

Hearing no follow-up questions or any new safety rules, I was good to go.

Back in the room, I found Ronnie shining my Dick Tracy flashlight into the tiny slot on top of the piggy bank. As if I didn't know where the coins were hiding, Ronnie excitedly pointed inside the bank, exclaiming, "Clink, clink."

With Ronnie holding the flashlight over the slot, I carefully placed the flat end of the butter knife into the bank and stirred it around, hoping something would pop out. Seeing one coin appear and then fall back inside the bank, it became clear. Since gravity helped put the coins in, reverse gravity would help get them out.

Lifting the bank over my head and turning it upside down, I began to shake it. Nothing came out. Gripping the butter knife, I slowly inserted the long flat edge into the slot and poked it around.

After 10 minutes, all I got was a nickel and three pennies. Seeing my lack of progress, Ronnie jumped up and ran out of the bedroom door, leaving me alone with my stingy smiling piggy bank. This was taking way too long.

Searching for a solution, I remembered the advice Nono gave me while sitting next to him on the porch steps. "Se la roccia è troppo grande, basta spezzarla."

Coming from a man who built stone houses with rocks dug out of his native land in northern Italy, it was brilliant. "If the rock is too big, just break it into smaller pieces."

With that simple bit of advice, my grandpa handed me the key to solving a lot of life's biggest problems. At the time, I had no idea when or where I would ever use it, but it was clear. The piggy bank was a big rock, and I needed to smash it into smaller pieces.

In a flash, I was at my dad's workbench. Digging through his toolbox, I found the perfect piggy bank break-in tool - a bright and shiny ball-peen hammer.

Running up the cellar and hallway stairs, taking them two at a time, I was back in my bedroom in no time. I slowly shut the door and turned to look at piggy, who appeared to look a bit frightened all of a sudden. Without a second thought, I moved into position, took aim, closed my eyes, and swung.

Bammmmm!

Taking a quick look at the wreckage strewn all over the bedroom floor, it was obvious why my piggy bank always felt overweight. Ronnie was feeding Piggy with any metal object that fit through the slot on its back. Coins, metal washers, brass locknuts, safety pins, earrings, and pieces of metal from Dad's workbench were mixed in with chunks of my once-upon-a-time perfect piggy bank.

With less than an hour to go before supper, I needed to toss out all the scrap pieces of metal, get Mom's earrings back in her bedroom, and glue the bank back together before putting back any money I didn't need.

With model airplane glue, rubber bands, and clear plastic tape, the piggy bank was miraculously back on my nightstand in one piece in less than thirty minutes. A big band-aid blocked most of the piggy's annoying smile, which was a small loss to an otherwise acceptable restoration.

As I looked at my masterpiece, Ronnie burst through the doorway and was about to say something when he spotted the stacks of coins next to the repaired piggy bank. Pointing to the pile of nickels, he immediately demanded, "My turn. My turn!"

"Just dimes, nickels, and pennies this time! That's all. Got it?" I commanded. Ronnie enthusiastically shook his head, yes.

Grabbing the nickel from my hand, Ronnie placed it over the open slot as I held my breath, hoping the piggy bank would stay in one piece after it hit bottom.

Looking straight at me, Ronnie gave his signature pre-drop announcement, "Clink. Clink!" A split second after the coin was released, Piggy gave his own reply in an alarming off-note tone of voice – "*CLUNK!*"

A disappointed frown clouded Ronnie's face. "Clunk?" he offered, wondering if he had heard the sound correctly. Like a concerned doctor listening to a patient's chest, he immediately provided his diagnosis, "Piggy bant broktid." Ronnie dropped the other coins, frowned, and went off to wash up for dinner.

It was clear. The operation to repair Piggy did not meet Ronnie's approval. On the positive side of things, I knew Mom would love seeing her earrings again, Dad would have extra washers to fix stuff, and Ronnie would not be doing any more banking at this location ever again.

Chapter Five
The Big Bang Strikes Again!

With an entire library of
comic books at my disposal,
it wasn't hard to dismiss my
parent's explanation of how a
flying stork was strong enough
to deliver my pudgy 9-pound,
diaper-clad body to a crib inside
their house.

Instead, I was pretty sure that
I had been beamed aboard Planet Earth sometime after the 13.7
billionth birthday of the Big Bang. In recorded Earth history,
this would put my arrival somewhere between the last week of
February and the first week of March 1947.

The reason I couldn't pin down my exact delivered-on date
had to do with my parents' scheme to throw a joint birthday
party for Ronnie and me somewhere between our actual arrival
dates. To keep both of us confused, my parents never revealed
our exact birthdays, no matter how hard we tried. Whose
birthday came first was anybody's guess.

"Boys. Get ready for your big party next Sunday."

Fishing for any small clue, every year, I tried to catch my
mom off guard, "Mom. Can't we have it on my real birthday
day this time?"

My mom smiled. "It wouldn't be fair. It's this Sunday, and that's that."

I wanted to say, *What day was I delivered on exactly? Not fair to whom exactly?*

Of course, I didn't press the issue for fear of being looked upon as being disrespcctful or ungrateful, resulting in canceling the entire party. Besides, I didn't want to blow my cover by appearing too nosey.

Believe me when I tell you, not knowing your actual birthday is bad enough, but having a delivered-on day so close to your own brother, well, that comes with lots of downsides. Let me explain why in just two simple words: Joint gifts.

"Oh, look. Here's one from your Auntie Elsa and Uncle Aldo for both of you. Say, thank you." Mom would instruct Ronnie and me as she handed us the beautifully wrapped gift with its double blue bow and ribbons.

In the time it took to say, "Thank you, Auntie and Uncle." we ripped off the ribbons, bows, wrapping paper, and already opened the box, all at breathtaking speed.

"I get to play first!"

"No, me!"

Custody battles over joint toys, including my favorite Howdy Doody doll or the toy firetruck with its working firehose, went on for years. Mom could have gotten a law degree from all the times she worked out temporary visitation rights to settle our daily disputes.

Besides joint gifts, we were doomed to share the same birthday cake, candles, photos, balloons, party favors, and decorations on a day that never coincided with either of our "delivered-on" dates, whatever they might be.

"Ok, boys. Blow out the candles." Mom's voice boomed over the din of cousins, parents, aunts, uncles and friends.

Just as I was taking in a big deep breath, I spotted Ronnie already in the process of blowing out all the candles. In a last-minute attempt to catch up, I let out the biggest baddest blast ever recorded in candle blowing history. Unfortunately, instead of quickly extinguishing flames, my Category 5 hurricane-force gust encountered the remanents of smoke rising above a small field of smoldering candle stakes left behind after Ronnie's surprise attack.

As Dad's camera caught Ronnie's triumphant smile, there I was captured on film for all time in a silly, eyes shut, lips fluttering second place-finish as everyone else appeared happy, laughing and joyful all around us.

"Foiled again," I mumbled to myself, with arms folded, trying to figure out what just happened.

As the cake was cut and scoops of ice cream were dished out, I resolved that next year, I would strike the first blow. For now, I'd just smile, have a good time, eat a lot of cake and ice cream, and hope the photo never made it into the family album.

Chapter Six
You Could Call Me Fearless!

By the time I was 8 years old, my friends had already pinned me with a bunch of nicknames. The most popular were Fast Freddy, Freddo, Stretch, and Fearless. It was the last nickname that made me cringe the most.

I admit, the nickname "Fearless" sounds pretty cool. Unfortunately, it came from the adventures of a character named Fearless Fosdick, a clueless, bumbling, crime-fighting police officer in the _Li'l Abner_ Sunday comic strip. He was funny and clever, alright, but he really wasn't too smart. For that reason, it bothered me a lot when kids yelled, "Hey, Fearless. You wanna play?"

"My name is Fredd with two d's." I'd yell back.

It might sound odd yelling, "with two d's!" every time the subject of my name came up, but I was determined to squelch all references to a blundering cartoon character who had no idea what was going on.

I'd like to say "Fredd with two d's" was all my idea, but I'll come clean - it really wasn't. I stumbled on the name while watching the _Captain Midnight_ TV show. During every episode, Captain Midnight's sidekick would explain to everyone he met, "My name is Ichabod Mudd. That's Mudd with two d's."

Bingo. With a name like Fredd with two d's, people just had to sit up and take notice. So, to get it just right, I started practicing in front of my mom's mirror.

"What's your name, son?" I'd say in a deep grownup's voice.

"Oh, that would be Fredd with two d's, sir," pumping my right arm in the air twice for emphasis. Unfortunately, it never did work out as well as planned.

No matter how hard I tried, grownups would hear my name and break into a bread commercial jingle that went something like this, "Bring Home the Butternut Bread, Fred. Yes. Bring Home the Butternut Bread." It was on at least ten times a day on both radio and TV.

Because of that popular commercial, whenever grown-ups saw me, they *never* thought, "Oh, that's the smart boy with two d's at the end of his name." Nope. Instead, whenever they saw me, they'd be reminded of their weekly grocery list.

But that's not the reason I eventually stopped saying "Fredd with two d's" It had to do with how my mom would introduce me. "Yes. My son's name is Frederick. You know, after Frederick the Great, who was the ruler of Austria."

What confused me wasn't the fact that my mom bragged on how she picked out my name, or that it had a royal ring to it, or that my namesake lived in a time before <u>mimeograph machines</u>. It was nothing like that at all.

Mostly it was knowing that unlike Frederick the Great, I was expected to take out the garbage, wash dishes, and polish the furniture. All the things he never had to do, because he had a sister named Wilhelmine.

Besides all that, I didn't live in a big castle like Frederick the Great did. Don't get me wrong. Our house was very nice, sitting on a pleasant avenue with big Dutch Elm trees overarching a picturesque street. But instead of a castle, we lived on the second story above my grandparents at 1362 Willow Avenue, overlooking McGrath and Durk's storage yard to the east, the Willow Inn Tavern to the south, and an alley to the north.

According to my mom, where a person lived didn't make them great or not. In fact, my mom made it clear that as rich as Frederick the Great was, all his subjects still loved him. He was a strong leader who had a good sense of humor and played the violin. Not your ordinary run-of-the-mill monarch.

If my mom's highest expectation was for me to be like Frederick the Great, I supposed maybe if I developed a good sense of humor, she might let the rest of his talents slide.

No such luck. Since Frederick the Great played the violin, my mom decided that I needed to play the violin - which brings me to my dad.

My dad was one of the first radar operators during WWII and flew in the radar/navigator seat on a Boeing B-29 Superfortress bomber. Once the war ended, my dad took his weekend pass and went straight to Paris, France, with his buddies. There he purchased a beautiful deep mahogany-stained violin and horsehair bow, complete with a velvet case, from a shop near the Eiffel Tower.

If you looked closely enough through one of the F-shaped holes on the top of the violin, you could spot the name Stradivarius along with the year 1736, written in ink. I didn't know if that meant it was a good violin or that it was the name of the original owner.

I guessed since it didn't say "Return for reward," it was ok for me to keep it. Just to make sure, I crossed out "Stradivarius" and scribbled, "Fredd's Violin, 1957," so there wouldn't be any confusion.

Every Saturday, rain or shine, my mom chauffeured me to violin classes in our 1956 De Soto. It was big with a stylish, high tailfin design and curb feelers to protect the whitewall tires. It looked like it could take off at any minute, even with the engine off.

The car was two-tone, red on top and white on the bottom, and had a push-button gear changer with the letters D-N-L-R on the dashboard next to the steering wheel.

Watching Mom get in, adjust the rearview mirror, start the engine, and push the D button, it dawned on me - D was for Day-time driving. Those folks at De Soto thought of everything.

I should point out that in my neighborhood, geeky kids were always fair game for big kids to pick on. That was even truer if they played violin in music class and carried books home from school.

So even though I wasn't too bad at playing the violin, I learned I was even better at running away from the neighborhood big kids with my violin case in one hand and a school bookbag in the
other. Let's just say, if "Violin with School Bag Sprint" was an event, I would make the U.S. team hands down.

After two years of school and private violin lessons, my best piece was "America the Beautiful." Unfortunately, not everybody appreciated my talent.

"Hey, Joey. Guess what. My mom said people had tears in their eyes when I was playing 'America the Beautiful!'"

"Sure, mostly because all that loud, screeching noise hurt everybody's ears." That was not the kind of honest critique a violinist wants to hear from his best friend, especially after hours of practice.

One day, long after she lost all hope of having a violin-playing ruler in the family, my mom decided to tie a green ribbon around its thin wooden neck and hang it high above our family room fireplace as a decoration.

31

Looking at it hanging there in silent exile, I couldn't help but feel guilty. Had I somehow been a violin-playing ruler of a powerful country, it would have had a place of honor hanging over a much bigger and fancier fireplace somewhere in a bustling castle with a view of the Alps.

Story Two
A Gremlin in the Attic

Chapter One
Area 51

As time went by, I could not find a single photo, drawing, newspaper account, or any clue that would support the idea that I had been beamed aboard Planet Earth. The distinct lack of evidence led me to another possible explanation - I had crash-landed here by accident - like a pothole on a transgalactic trip.

In fact, it was Joey's *DC Comics* first edition of *Superboy* that helped me figure out how it must have happened. If Clark Kent could crash-land his spaceship in a field near Smallville, Kansas, it wasn't a farfetched idea  to think I crashed into the small open lot right across the street from my parent's house in Niagara Falls, New York. Anybody could see it was the perfect spot for an emergency landing.

Sure - I was lucky to survive a harrowing intergalactic trip - but the crash was so bad that it damaged a sizable number of my preinstalled memory modules, making it necessary for me to attend a data retrieval center known as Cleveland Avenue Elementary School. Why else would I need to go there?

All I had to do was figure out how my parents got me out of the spaceship without tipping off the neighbors, and also answer the big question - what did they do with it?

If they didn't bury it in the field, it was a sure bet it had to be in the creepy attic just off the short hallway outside our second-floor kitchen. Just a quick glance at the door made me shudder. The prospect of rummaging through that spooky attic all by myself gave me the willies.

To make matters worse, the attic was declared a restricted area the day my dad warned me, "Fred. Never go into the attic. It's off-limits. Understand?" That order made me a lot more curious about what was really up there. Even so, it was clear. For now, I'd have to do all my snooping around without so much as setting one foot inside the attic.

One morning, while sitting on the porch steps with my grandpa, I decided to push forward with my investigation. "Nono. What's up in the attic?"

Nono began puffing on his wooden pipe like a train going up a steep mountain. Suddenly Nono stopped and looked sideways at me. Using words in the language he learned in the old country, Nono shook his finger 'NO!' and then pointing in the direction of the attic door, he cautioned, "No go zu scala, è proibito su attica un signore gremlin vive."

To underscore his point, Nono touched his head and waved his finger again in the universal "Don't even think about it" sign language message.

Bingo. That told me all I needed to know. From my limited Tyrolean vocabulary, I now understood that my grandpa agreed with my dad, except Grandpa Nono explained why. The attic was forbidden territory because a gremlin lived there, and he really DID NOT like kids.

I began to digest what my grandpa said. First off, I didn't know what this gremlin person looked like, but I knew I didn't want to cross paths with him.

So, not only did I not want to go up in the attic, but now I'd have to keep a sharp eye out in case signor gremlin decided to use the hallway stairs to go to the basement.

It was then that it hit me. There was no other plausible explanation. This gremlin person had been hired by my parents to keep me from snooping around the house in search of my spaceship. That had to be it, but now what?

It was the week after my grandpa's warning that Joey appeared with a 1/64th scale Atlas model rocket he had just bought from Ace Hobby Shop. After setting out all the pieces on my kitchen table, Joey began applying glue to the edges of the rocket nose cone while I tried to read the assembly instructions. "Hey, Fred. Can we go play in your attic?"

Dropping the instruction sheet like a hot potato, I immediately shot a glance past Joey, visualizing the entrance to the attic just beyond the closed kitchen door to my right. Beads of sweat began rolling down my forehead as I searched frantically for the best response that wouldn't frighten Joey.

"Well, I, uh. No, we can't because there's kind of ah, like ah, a gremlin person who lives up there, and he doesn't much like kids."

There, I said it. A secret I'd been keeping to myself for weeks, in fear of having friends find out and avoid coming over to my house to play.

Seeing my distress, Joey took on a casual tone of voice. "That's nothing. I have one in the attic and one in the basement. There are two gremlins in my house. You only got one!"

A feeling of instant relief washed over me. I learned at that moment that the mark of a good friend is someone who can cut your problem in half by pointing out just how lucky you were that it wasn't twice as bad as it could have been.

Joey added, "My dad, Aunt Helen, and my grandpa warned me."

"Really?" I said, feeling a lot better now that the secret was out. Best of all, my best friend wasn't scared at all, so why should I be? I straightened up and stood shoulders back, looking in the direction of the attic door.

Joey could see he was helping me a lot with my problem, so he pushed on. "Yeah. Besides, we can wait until he gets bored and moves out. Then we can go up and play in the attic any time we want."

Joey's idea was great. If I could make it really boring in

my house, the unwanted house guest might decide to quit and move out before Christmas.

Unfortunately, with my brother, two puppies, a goldfish, my parents, grandparents, and all kinds of relatives and friends coming over all the time, it was going to be an uphill battle.

I needed a Plan B.

Chapter Two
Santa's Watching!

Each morning, Mom would deliver a barrage of safety messages, accompanied by a menacing index finger hitting the air above my head for emphasis, "Go straight to school! Don't talk to strangers. Make sure you walk with Joey!" and the all-important, "Look both ways before crossing the street!"

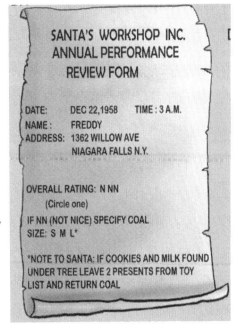

SANTA'S WORKSHOP INC.
ANNUAL PERFORMANCE
REVIEW FORM

DATE: DEC 22,1958   TIME : 3 A.M.
NAME :   FREDDY
ADDRESS: 1362 WILLOW AVE
           NIAGARA FALLS N.Y.

OVERALL RATING: N NN
     (Circle one)
IF NN (NOT NICE) SPECIFY COAL
SIZE: S M L*

*NOTE TO SANTA: IF COOKIES AND MILK FOUND
UNDER TREE LEAVE 2 PRESENTS FROM TOY
LIST AND RETURN COAL

Mom's last words were always, "Now run, or you'll be late!"

If we disobeyed any of these orders, it was a known fact that Santa Claus would somehow find out which wasn't good because you could end up on the wrong side of Santa's gift list – the lumps of coal side - before you knew what hit you.

To stay on Santa's good side, you needed to be a <u>Dudley Do-Right</u>, righting wrongs, helping damsels in distress, being forthright, honest, and never tell a lie. In fact, if you so much as told a fib, sure enough, Santa would know. It was kind of creepy.

In fact, any incident – good or bad - would appear on

Santa's annual performance evaluation form along with detailed instructions on which toys to drop off, cross-indexed by home address. An 'NN" (Not Nice) grade meant Santa would leave at least one lump of coal, that is, unless he found cookies and milk waiting for him under the tree. For that reason, I always left a stack of cookies and a big glass of cold milk as extra insurance <u>every</u> Christmas Eve.

The weeks before the big day were magical. Sitting around the kitchen table, my dad would break into his favorite rendition of "Santa Claus is Coming to Town." Mom would add her own version, singing out every note in her high soprano opera voice, accompanied by Hawaiian Hula dance hand movements for added effect.

"I'm telling you once, and I'm telling you nice. Don't you scurry like little mice ....BECAUSE......If you wash the dirty dishes, Santa will fill all your Christmas wishes! So don't you fret and don't delay. Santa's watching and filling his sleigh!"

Jumping down from the kitchen table, Ronnie moved his chair to the sink, demanding, "My turn. I wash. You dry!"

"No, it's my turn." I shot back, pulling his chair over to the front of the drying rack.

"Boys. Santa's watching." Mom was in no mood for another after dinner, 'I wash, you dry' argument. "Settle it now," she said with her arms folded across her chest.

"<u>Rock-paper-scissors,</u>" Ronnie announced, jumping to face me eyeball to eyeball. There was no better way to settle a good old fashioned dispute than with a rock-paper-scissors duel.

Standing toe-to-toe with my shooting hand behind my back, I had a premonition that Ronnie would shoot out his hand in the symbol for scissors, and since rock always breaks scissors, I chose the clenched fist symbol for a rock. I was ready to win.

In unison, we chanted, "One, two, three, shoot!"

Looking at our outstretched hands, I was shocked. Ronnie went for the paper sign, displaying a flat open hand with palm pointing down to the floor. "I win!" Ronnie shouted. "Paper covers rock. You dry."

Ronnie grinned in triumph and moved the chair to the left. Dishwashing always took a lot longer when my brother got to wash, but with Santa watching, I didn't say another word.

As we got older, Ronnie told me that he suspected Santa's spies were none other than Mom and Dad. I, on the other hand, had a different conspiracy theory. I figured the real spy in the ointment was that pesky old gremlin person. From his attic hideout, he could easily use my spaceship's radio to report everything directly to the North Pole. We'd never know.

Still in all, for all the spies and conspiracy theories, I miraculously never saw a speck of coal in my stocking on Christmas morning. That was the good news. Sadly, it was a sure sign from my haul of two toys and a year's worth of clothing, that if I really wanted more toys, I needed to move up from the basic but acceptable 'Nice' category to the lofty designation of a 'Very Nice' exemplary kid who deserved everything he asked for.

The thought of kids all over the world working on their own performance-improvement plans kept me up nights wondering how I could be nicer. I was already maxed out, like, for instance, the time I even gave Ronnie my prized <u>Mickey Mantle</u> baseball card, which he proceeded to use as a <u>bicycle noisemaker</u>. Of course, since Joey chewed a lot of gum, I knew he had at least two of every New York Yankee player since Babe Ruth. Maybe I would convince him to trade Mickey for my brother. Mom probably would nix the deal anyway.

So, if all the kids in the world worked at being a lot nicer than me, what could I possibly do to convince Santa that I deserved more toys, especially when I knew, being nicer wasn't going to be easy. For one thing, my brother's "little kid" status in the neighborhood was sure to do me in.

It's kind of complicated but, just think of Ronnie as "Rudolph" in the song "Rudolph the Red-Nosed Reindeer." My friends would be the reindeers named Dasher, Dancer, Prancer, Vixen, Comet, Cupid, Donner, and Blitzen. Even though Ronnie didn't have a red nose, he was four years younger than my friends and me, so Bobby, Ty, Carly, Danny, Davey, Billy, Richie, and Rodney would not let Ronnie play in any "big" kids games.

Every day, summer, fall, winter, and spring, I had to decide between playing with my brother or playing with my friends. That was a lot of pressure for a kid who had his eyes set on one awesome toy for Christmas.

It was a Gilbert Erector set No. 12 "Mysterious Walking Robot" complete with a battery-powered motor, and lights for eyes. Sure, being kind always had its own rewards, but the possibility of snagging a Christmas present I really wanted just meant I needed to go that extra mile you always hear about even though nobody tells you how long it takes to finish the trip.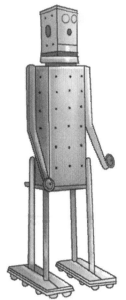

So to make my case on August 1st of each year, I would send a letter addressed to 'Santa, North Pole' with pages of handwritten stories detailing all the good deeds I had done, starting with how I always did the dishes for Mom and ending with something nice I did for my brother. I even included a crayon picture of the stack of cookies and carrots that would be waiting once Santa and his reindeer got to our house.

While watching Mom fill out her <u>S&H Green Stamps</u> order form, I had a brainstorm. Why not ask what Santa wants for Christmas!

"Dear Santa. Ronnie and I hope the reindeer liked the carrots we left next to the goodies for you. In addition to my usual list of toys this year, I have included a cookie order form for you. If you have a favorite cookie, please circle it on the form and leave the list by the fireplace. My mom says she'll help me bake them for your next visit. Thanks, and I hope to see you again soon! Sincerely yours, Freddy and Ronnie. P.S. Watch out for the new <u>TV antenna</u> Dad just attached to our chimney. Be careful! Signed, *Sincerely, Fredd*."

Still, it was puzzling. For all my past efforts, I continued to get toys that were not anywhere on my list. It was obvious. Something wasn't right. Joey, on the other hand, got all the toys he wanted. I needed to know how he did it.

After one Christmas, Joey and I were outside throwing snowballs at icicles hanging from gutters on his grandparents' house. In between packing snowballs, I shot him a question. "Joey, I don't get it. I was super nice to Ronnie all year, and I wrote to Santa and explained about the walking robot toy. I bet he never got my letter."

"Nah. Santa has lots of helpers. They'd never lose your letter." Just then, Joey winged a snowball at the biggest icicle I had ever seen. Direct hit. Freed from the gutter, the spike of ice crashed into the driveway. It was a perfect shot. Glistening pieces  of ice bounced off the pavement in every direction, covering the driveway between the two houses.

Looking up at the roof for his next target, Joey asked a simple question, "Did you use two stamps? I always use two stamps on my letters to Santa."

To my horror, Joey had just figured out my problem faster than a bobsled running full speed down an ice-covered hill headed for a cliff.

"Two stamps?" I stammered.

"And did you include a return address?" He asked in a helpful tone of voice.

If his letter required two stamps, then mine needed ten! This past summer alone, I spent at least a week pasting together multipage lists for Santa, complete with drawings of the toy robot. For the other toys, I neatly folded and taped each handprinted toy name, with different colored arrows pointing to a corresponding photo on the page that I had carefully cut out of my mom's Sears, Roebuck and Company Catalog.

Joey only used a No. 2 pencil and one piece of paper!

"Two stamps." I stammered again, feeling more and more carsick over my letter's humiliating fate, sadly coming up way short of its planned thousand-mile trip to the North Pole.

Joey's analysis was a big kick in the toy chest and a bigger lesson on the importance of leaving nothing to chance when it came to sending letters to Santa's Workshop. It was lucky I got any toys from Santa at all and even luckier, I never tried to send back all the broken toys for new ones. They would never have made it.

When I sent my next letter, I knew what to do. I'd use two stamps for sure.

Chapter Three
Saturday Morning Test Patterns

My dad built our first TV set using a war surplus oscilloscope, 12-inch speaker, aluminum chassis, and an amplifier powered by <u>vacuum tubes</u>. Every Saturday morning, Ronnie and I would get up early, turn on the power switch, squat on the floor, and fix our eyes on the black and white TV screen just three feet in front of us.

Within seconds, we found ourselves locked in another blinking contest with a rugged Indian Chief in full ceremonial headdress. Around the Chief's head were four circles, with a bunch of numbers and lines inside each one. Week after week, the Chief never flinched.

With a good ten minutes before the start of the <u>TV broadcast day</u>, we had nothing better to do than to stand our ground and stare back. The good news was that instead of <u>snow on the TV screen</u>, we had something to look at while we waited. The bad news was that it didn't take long for the Chief to temporarily burn his overpowering likeness onto our eyeballs.

At exactly 8 a.m., the Chief finally disappeared. A few seconds later, big black letters appeared as a disembodied TV announcer belted out his spine-tingling introduction for *The Lone Ranger*.

Dressed in cowboy style pajamas, Ronnie and I sang along with the announcer, raising and lowering our voices in perfect harmony as he detailed the legend of the Lone Ranger, his Horse, Silver, and faithful Indian companion, Tonto, and how they fought for law and order in the old west.

It was inspiring, exciting, and thrilling all at the same time. By the final, "Hi-Yo Silver!" Ronnie and I were transported back in time, ready to relive the entire adventure. Yessiree. We were geared up and riding alongside our hero, experiencing everything through our very own 10-inch porthole view of the wild west.

By the first cereal commercial, the Chief's face that had superimposed itself on our vision was finally gone from our sight. In spite of an overpowering urge to eat large bowls of Kix, we stayed glued to the TV in the event the Lone Ranger and Tonto needed to deputize us to catch the bad guys.

One particularly cold and overcast Saturday morning, Ronnie and I took our usual places in front of the television set. Ronnie had his favorite blankie pinned tightly under his arm so I couldn't grab it from him. Not that I'd want to. I had given up needing a blankie months ago and was just as happy to haul Trigger, my stuffed horse, around for moral support.

Fifteen minutes before the TV broadcast day was about to start, I reached up and flicked on the power. To our shock and dismay, the Indian Chief's head suddenly began to roll up to the top, followed by another image of the Chief emerging from the bottom, following right behind in hot pursuit. Ronnie and I bobbed our heads up and down as we tracked each picture of the Chief, over and over again. It almost looked like the Chief had gotten a war party together and outnumbered us 10 to 1.

Ronnie finally gasped in dismay, "You broke it."

Ronnie's accusation shook me out of my trance. "Hold your horses, pardner," I replied in a half daze now fully under the hypnotic spell caused by the Chief's rolling screen image.

Another good three minutes went by. No amount of wishful thinking made it stop. Ronnie again broke the trance with three simple words. "Fix it now!"

Ronnie was right. Because I was four years older, I should possess advanced skills that could remedy the situation. I could, after all, adjust the volume, contrast, and brightness knobs on the front of the TV, so I did have some valuable technical know-how.

Unfortunately, I knew the controls for "Vertical Hold" and "Horizontal Hold" were on the back panel, a virtual no man's land that even gremlins stayed away from unless they went to TV school. Dad had shown me those critical control knobs before issuing Safety Lecture Number 121. It was a strong, almost Biblical warning, "Never touch the back of the TV set. Never. It will be curtains for you and your TV shows if you do.".

There was no other option. We had to get Dad's help or risk watching the Lone Ranger ride up the TV screen instead of across.

Using my birth order seniority, I turned to Ronnie and demanded, "You go wake up, Dad."

Even with my four years of family member seniority, Ronnie quickly figured out that I wasn't part of management. As far as he was concerned, we were both equals, hanging on to the last rung of the family's organizational ladder. As a result, Ronnie didn't feel compelled to listen to anything I said, especially if it could land him in trouble.

"Am not." Ronnie shot back.

"Are too," I yelled in reply, trying to sound like management material.

"What's going on?" My dad's groggy voice made us jump. Negotiations were over. Like it or not, we were now dealing with upper management.

"The test pattern. It's rolling." I blurted out. Dad didn't seem pleased to know I could speak in advanced TV troubleshooting jargon this early in the morning. Without reply, Dad unceremoniously shut the TV off, turned to look at us, and gave us a lecture on test pattern watching I'll never forget.

"You boys are going to hurt your eyes if you keep staring at that test pattern. Go do something else for ten minutes. Now!"

Without hesitation, we ran off to our bedroom, closed the

door, and stared at the clock on the wall. The key was to follow Dad's orders without any hint of resistance or hesitation. So for 10 minutes straight, Ronnie and I sat there glued to the floor, watching the secondhand go around the clock face over and over again.

When the big hand finally landed straight up on the number 12, and the little hand was on the 8, we shot out of our room like two cannonballs aimed squarely at the TV's power switch.

Beating Ronnie to the knob, I twisted it. Hearing the familiar 'click,' we didn't think so much as to breathe as the set warmed up with a faint humming noise. Finally, an unsymmetrical white dot magically appeared at the center of the screen. The elastic electronic blob quickly expanded to fill the picture tube screen with the words, 'The Lone Ranger" stretched across it.

Dad had fixed it. No roll and no pesky test pattern images anywhere in view. Our dad, the genius, was right again. While waiting for any show to start, a wall clock is much better to stare at than a test pattern.

For all that drama, TV watching was off-limits during school days. Reading books filled up hours of free time waiting for the weekend. In the meantime, I would mark the days until the next bookmobile truck arrived at our school.

A bookmobile was like a roving extension of the city library building, only better. The interior was about the size of a city bus, but in place of passenger seats, there were shelves

49

loaded with books, lining each exterior wall. It even had its own <u>Dewey Decimal System</u> card catalog that helped you find books on any subject.

From where I sat in school, I could spot the bookmobile rolling to a stop in the parking lot near the playground. When it arrived, Mrs. Nelson announced, " Ok, class. Line up at the door, single file. The bookmobile is here."

Once inside the bookmobile, I would make my way to the card catalog, and track down science fiction books like *Horton Hears a Who!* by Dr. Seuss, or books with a lot fewer pictures like Jules Verne's *From the Earth to the Moon* or H.G. Wells' book *The War of the Worlds*. Great stuff for a kid believing that someday he'd be vacationing on the moon and attending college on Mars.

It was a perfect system, except for the steep penalty for returning books that went past their due date. Basically, if you missed the due date, you owed the library money. There were even stories on TV about people getting arrested in small towns for not paying their fines on overdue books.

What I couldn't figure out was, if reading was so important to learning stuff, why did borrowing books have to be so expensive and stressful? Most of the time, they just sat on shelves gathering dust anyway.

Believe me when I tell you, in the

1950s, anything over a dollar was a lot of money. Two days after checking out a book from the library, I started having nightmares about forgetting them. It was always the same. A strict looking librarian would appear from behind a big wooden desk with a cashbox sitting right in the middle between us. "Ok, Fred. That's forty days you are late, times three books, times two-cents per book. That will be $2.40, please, and we don't take deposit bottles!"

Even with the nightmares, I often forgot about them, so I was kind of lucky that Mom had a sixth sense about late library books. Every Saturday morning she'd say, "Frederick. There are dust bunnies covering the big pile of books under your bed. I hope they aren't overdue again!"

To which I replied, "Uh, Mom? Can you drive me to the library? My bike's got a flat." I believed driving there might somehow make the books less late than they already were.

"You know, walking never hurt anybody. Take your brother and scoot." My mom grew up somewhere on the highest peaks of the Alps, so my mile walk on perfectly level ground, free of dangerous cliffs or rock slides, gave way to exactly no sympathy nor any understanding at all.

As I trudged out the side door, three overdue books in hand, all I could think of was, where were the rocket-propelled scooters when you needed them?

Chapter Four
It's All About the Fish

A lot of times, I'd ride my bike
to The Falls just for fun. While most
people saw tons of water flowing
by, I saw a great spot to go fishing.
Think about it. Every day, there had
to be tons of fish taking their final
ride over the brink of the falls. Plain

and simple, it was the perfect fishing hole, but no one knew it.

The big question was how do you catch a fish flying by at 30 miles an hour? A bobber and a hook wouldn't do it. Casting off idea after idea, it finally hit me. Don't use a fishing pole. No. Use a big net instead!

The thought hooked my imagination and wouldn't let go. I could snag a zillion fish in seconds. No hours of waiting for just one nibble. They'd be caught faster than 1-2-3 and pan-fried to perfection on our new electric stove in minutes.

As the idea sank in, I began to plan a simple contraption that would do the trick. I even watched my favorite TV science program, *The Mr. Wizard Show,* looking for an 'e-fish-ent' way (pun intended) to design my 'Fearless Fredd's Fabulous Fish-O-Rama Fishing Net.' It came down to finding some netting, seven wire clothes hangers, and a metal pole. That's it.

"Hey, mom. Where's the badminton net?"

Mom quickly answered the question adding a bit of her own exasperation in the bargain. "Did you look under the bed with all the rest of your toys?".

"Oh, yeah. Thanks, mom."

It wasn't that I was messy or anything like that. It was just that my brother Ronnie and I shared a bedroom, and our twin beds hugged the left and right walls with a neutral zone in between. Even though I was neater, we both stuffed as much as we could under our beds to make sure there wasn't any room for monsters to hide. You couldn't even fit a baseball under our beds, even if you shot it from a cannon.

Dropping to all fours, I began fishing around under my bed, pulling out one toy after another. It wasn't there. All I could figure was that the pesky gremlin person took it. Right or wrong, I blamed him for a lot of things.

Just then, my brother Ronnie appeared out of nowhere. "What ya looking for Fred?"

Ronnie was getting way better at English, so sign language wasn't needed. Besides, the pile of toys in the middle of our room made it obvious.

"Nothin' special. Just the badminton net. Where is it?" I inquired in a bossy big brother tone of voice.

Ronnie shrugged his shoulders, "I don't know."

Taking advantage of my floor-level position to expand the search, I quickly rolled along the floor towards Ronnie's bed, dodging Lincoln Logs, Tinker Toy parts, small trucks and, other toys that hadn't seen the light of day for years. After ten minutes of helping me dig, Ronnie exclaimed, "Got it," as he pulled out a tangled ball of red and white string.

Relieved that the gremlin person hadn't swiped it, I grabbed the crumpled up mess and ran to the basement, searching for dad's red <u>Naugahyde</u>-covered TV repairman's toolbox. Locating the secret latch that dad had installed to keep little kids out, I popped it open, located the roll of black tape under boxes of <u>vacuum tubes</u> and grabbed the pointy-nosed pliers.

Looking at the concrete laundry tub, I spotted my grandma's telescoping dining room curtain rod. It was perfect. By the time the curtains dried on the basement clothesline, I would have the curtain rod back before Nona even knew it was gone.

With all the needed materials and tools, it didn't take long to hook the edges of the cut-up net to the outstretched and modified ends of each coat hanger. In a jiffy, I was ready for a test!

The plan was simple. Using water flowing from the bathtub faucet to model the falls, a chair to simulate shoreline rocks, and a bathtub full of water for a mini gorge, I would recreate the conditions at the bottom of Niagara Falls fully outfitted to catch a mother load of fish!

After dragging my invention into the bathroom, I ran back and grabbed one of mom's dining room chairs and moved it just outsde the bathroom door. Quickly turning the bathtub faucet to full blast, I carefully placed Ronnie's rubber ducky in the center of the net for added realism. With a sense of mounting excitement, I climbed onto the chair, and began extending the net toward the watery deluge sprewing out a few feet in front of me.

It didn't take long to figure out that this was definitely going to be a bad idea.

As soon as the outstretched net hit the water, the rod jumped out of my hands, caroming off the medicine cabinet, before bouncing up, for its trip across the bathroom vanity, using its handle to wipe out every bottle, tube, toothbrush, comb, razor, and bar of soap in its path. It was a clean sweep.

Leaping from my perch, I hit the deck hard with both feet. A spray of water shot up from small pools of liquid merging into one big multicolored puddle. A quick glance revealed that my fishing net handle was kinked into the shape of the letter L. If that wasn't bad enough, mom's makeup mirror and a bottle of perfume were on the floor too. The only good news was that nothing looked broken.

Just when I thought it

was safe to breathe, an overwhelming smell of flowers filled the room, growing stronger by the second. Mom's favorite bottle of perfume was intact, alright but the cap was missing and half the bottle was empty!

I had an even bigger problem on my hands. During all the action, my miniature gorge was spilling over the bathtub and onto the bathroom floor. With just seconds to stop the flood from hitting the hallway, I sprung into action.

As I reached for the drain plug, a tidal wave of water leaped over the bathtub rim and onto the floor. It seemed to take forever before I could fully shut off the water.

Wet from head to toe, I began sopping up the large puddle of water and perfume swirling around my feet. Wringing towel after wet towel down the sink when it was over, the floor sparkled and never smelled so good.

As I made my way to the hallway <u>laundry chute</u>, a trail of water drops marked my path. Jamming the soaking wet towels through the small door, I listened as they slid all the way slowly down, ending with a loud "thunk" before they dropped into the dirty clothes box in the basement. They made it. "Out of sight. Out of mind," I mumbled to myself.

Except everything had to be out of sight and out of smell! I knew mom would begin a grand inquisition the next time she needed her Azurest Perfume. Replacing the cap on the bottle of perfume, I had a brilliant idea.

What if I invented a new fragrance?" I exclaimed out loud.

"That's it!" I had hours of practice under my belt, mixing up strange concoctions in my effort to find a cure for my brother's diaper rash. How hard could it be to make a new perfume scent for mom? She might like it, and I'd be off the hook.

OK, I thought. *This is basic chemistry. I can figure this out. Maybe kerosene or turpentine or something from my dad's workshop in the basement would do the trick.*

Looking around, I saw something that was even better. Grabbing dad's bottle of peppermint flavored mouthwash, I filled the Azurest Perfume bottle to the top. It turned from a pleasant blue to the exact color of antifreeze and smelled just a little like, well, like peppermint-scented flowers.

Not bad, really. Mom would be proud of me too. Of course, I might have to move to Paris and give up fishing at The Falls, but I could live with that.

Shoving everything else back on top of the vanity, I grabbed Nona's curtain rod and ran down to the basement. Except for a small, slightly noticeable kink, it was almost back to its original shape. With just a few more things to do, it looked like any evidence of my failed experiment would be hard to dig up, that is if it weren't for one tiny detail - Today was laundry day.

Bounding off the last basement step, I immediately spotted mom holding a bunch of wet towels. Failing to complete a full mid-air U-turn, there was nothing else to do but stumble across the basement floor.

As the scent of Azurest Perfume hung heavy in the basement

air and with the damaged curtain rod in my possession, it didn't look good for the soon-to-be-famous inventor of the Fish-O-Rama fishing net. I had to say something fast.

"But mom, I can explain."

"Oh. I'm listening."

"The gremlin did it!"

"Sure, and the dust bunnies under your bed bent Nona's curtain rod. Right?" Mom wasn't buying it.

I was holding onto the anchor of a sinking ship, and I knew it. With animated hand motions, I explained my invention and the brilliant test plan, throwing in how the next design would work for sure, and that now she had a new full bottle of peppermint-scented antifreeze colored Azurest Perfume that I had invented just for her.

"It will really smells great, mommy. Wait until you smell it!"

Mom still wasn't swallowing any part of my fishing-net-that-got-away-but-it-is-all-good-really story. Exhausted from listening to all my apologies and plans to redesign my fishing net, mom sighed, "Get the cleaning supplies, clean up your mess, and stop blaming the gremlin every time you get into trouble."

Having falsely accused the gremlin person in the attic, mom added, "And make sure you see Father Glynn for confession. Honestly, Frederick."

The next day I told Joey that I needed to fess up to Father Glynn. Joey was oddly happy about my predicament. "Hey, I might slip up. You never know. So sure, I'll go if you go too." Joey seemed truly happy to walk the plank with me.

"Are you sure?" I replied.

Joey confirmed it. "Yeah. What are best friends for? I mean, right?"

In certain life situations, like going to confession, its always best to have a friend you can count on to make sure you don't chicken out.

Chapter Five
My Friend the Saint

Saturday afternoon came
fast that week. Before going
inside the church, Joey and I
had to figure out who would
be second in line. After
three rounds of rock-paper-
scissors, I miraculously won,
meaning Joey would break
the ice with his list of fibs and
stuff, then I'd come sailing
in, right behind him, just an
average kid like Joey possibly
looking more like an angel in
comparison.

Once inside the church, Joey and I got in line behind at least
a dozen people. We inched our way along the pews toward the
confessional door with its lettered sign "Fr. Glynn" just below
a gleaming red light and a small sign announcing that Father
Glynn was on duty.

In no time, it was Joey's turn.

As Joey opened the door to go in, I looked at the clock on
the wall. It read 3:42 PM. I figured I had at least 5 to 6 minutes
to practice what I needed to say. "That's plenty of time," I
reassured myself. Joey blessed himself and went in.

Before I knew it, I heard Joey's voice, "Your turn." Joey held the door open, waving me in with a big smile on his face. "I only got a Hail Mary," Joey whispered with a grin.

It had to be a record! Joey was in for maybe 10 seconds tops. Only an up and coming saint could get through confession that fast. For crying out loud, I wasn't even halfway through my list. No matter. Ready or not, it was my turn.

As I trudged to the open door, Joey tried to lighten my mood, "Break a leg!" I wasn't amused.

"Bless me, Father. I was here last week. I forgot my morning prayers on Monday only. I didn't brush my teeth when my mom told me three times. I told a fib on somebody to my mom once and bent my grandma's curtain rod, but I fixed it."

Sandwiched somewhere between a couple of minor offenses, I hoped the fib would just slide by without any further interrogation.

It didn't.

"Son. Who was it that you told this fib on?"

I spilled my guts out. I described my invention, how it knocked down some stuff and bent my Nona's curtain rod, and how I pinned the rap on this gremlin kind of person who lives in the attic when all I wanted to do was catch fish.

"Did you say Mr. Gremlin?" Father Glynn was trying to get to the bottom of my story.

"Yes, sir. I mean, no. He's a gremlin person is all. My parents told me. They said a gremlin person lives there, and I wasn't supposed to go up in the attic. My grandparents said so too. Oh, and I was nicer to my brother all this week, Father."

"Oh." Father Glynn said quietly, sounding a bit perplexed. There was a long pause. My ears were so hot they could have melted an igloo.

Father Glynn cleared his voice quietly before speaking again. "You say your parents and your grandparents told you this?" He apparently missed the part about being nice to my brother for one entire week.

I was getting nervous. "Yes, Father. But no. Not my grandma. No, she didn't."

"You know you are not supposed to lie or bear false witness against your neighbor."

"Well, Father. He isn't really my neighbor. He lives upstairs in the attic."

Father Glynn went on. "That's not the point. You should never intentionally tell a lie about anything or anybody. You must be truthful at all times. It is what a good boy does."

"Yes, Father," I replied, wishing I was somewhere else.

"Now, obey your parents and say ten Hail Marys and ten Our Fathers and make a good Act of Contrition."

"Yes, Father. Thanks!"

Leaving the confessional, I noticed the line had gotten a lot longer.

Walking quickly to the last pew, I pulled the kneeler down too fast. With a loud thud, it hit the floor, echoing throughout the church. "What kept ya?" Joey asked in a low whisper.

"It's a long story," I replied, adding a heads-up, "This might take a while."

Leaving the church with my best friend Joey, I felt a lot better about the entire matter. Even the long session with Father Glynn didn't seem so bad. Better still, if I ever crossed paths with Mr. Gremlin, at least now I could look him straight in the eye and not feel guilty about blaming him for something he didn't do.

I knew it was going to be tough keeping my nose clean until next Saturday, but I was working with a clean slate for now. I just needed to make it through church services on Sunday morning.

At least one good thing that came out of the entire event. Now I knew what to get Mom for her birthday - a hand-drawn card showing plans for my improved fishing net design along with another bottle of Azurest Perfume from the Pharmacy next to the hardware store on Joey's street. Of course, for Nona, I'd spring for a new curtain rod for Christmas. One that wouldn't bend so easily next time.

Story Three
The Rocket Club

Chapter One
Friends Are Friends, No Matter Who Is Best

Bobby, Rodney, Joey, and I hung out a lot mostly because of our interest in rockets. But of all the kids that I knew, like you probably guessed, Joey and I were best friends, hands down. If you saw Joey, there was a 99.9 percent chance you'd see me. If we didn't look *so* different, you might think we were twin brothers or at least born on the same day.

While Joey sported a crew style haircut that somehow made the freckles on his face look cool, I had a full head of hair parted on one side with no freckles anywhere. Joey's solid build and muscular arms made him look like he was born to be a football player, which he did do in high school. I, on the other hand, was lanky and outgrew my clothes as soon as I tried them on.

Whenever I was with Joey, I never worried about big kids in the neighborhood wanting to bully me. Joey didn't take guff from anybody and, he made sure everyone knew that he and I were best friends. It was like having a family member as a personal bodyguard. Besides all that, Joey was funny and loved the same fun stuff I did.

It probably was just pure and simple coincidence, but it was scary just how close our houses were to each other. When you considered how big the planet was, how many people there were, and the number of streets in a city, it was hard to imagine how only a backyard, an alley, and Linwood Avenue was all that separated the two of us. It had to be divine intervention.

We were, in fact, so close that Joey's Aunt Helen and my mom decided to take turns escorting us to our kindergarten class and making sure we didn't get distracted along the way. It wasn't hard to see why.

One route took us past four stores with penny candy, a hardware store with a friendly dog looking to play fetch, a pharmacy full of the latest comic books, sidewalks full of hopscotch courts, and a park with swings and slides along the way. The other route was just as bad as far as distractions go.

Either way you went, there was a big chestnut tree that marked the last block before the school. Each autumn, fallen chestnuts covered the street, leaving large polished mahogany-colored nuts on the ground inside thick green pods. They were excellent for perfecting our throwing skills in preparation for the spontaneous neighborhood snowball fights that sprung up all over town right after a good snow fall.

After months of supervised trips, my mom announced, "Frederick, you and Joey can walk to school starting tomorrow.

Go straight to school, and don't get into any trouble."

Joey and I couldn't believe our ears. We could be on our own and have fun all the way to school.

"OK, Mom." I blurted out confidently, all the while hoping that Joey would remember the way in the morning.

Bright and early the very next day, Joey and I met up at the corner of Linwood Avenue and 15th Street. Aunt Helen was nowhere to be seen. Without a trail guide leading the way, we cautiously set out on our first unaccompanied journey across a patchwork of concrete sidewalks and tree-covered streets, every bit as excited as we could be.

At each street corner, Joey and I paused to look at our surroundings. By agreeing on the next house that we needed to walk past, we set our course in that direction.

Things were going great until our feet stopped at an intersection a few blocks from the school. Joey looked at me, and I looked at him. Neither of us took command. Not daring to move in either direction, we both gazed up and down the street.

"Isn't that Mr. Wolf's house?" Joey asked, pointing to our right.

"Yeah. Nobody ever walks past Mr. Wolf's house, so we definitely didn't ever walk down that block." I replied.

Joey quickly concurred, "OK, left it is."

Thanks to Mr. Wolf, we were finally back on course.

With two blocks to go, Joey asked a question, "Hey, Fred. Wanna take a shortcut?"

Against my better judgment, I agreed, "Sure. Why not?" Each word carefully selected to display an air of confidence even as a faint voice in my head was yelling, "Are you kidding me! No! No! No way!"

As hard as I tried, I could not recognize the voice, so I shrugged and chose to ignore the warning altogether. "Let's go."

Halfway down the alley, it was clear we should turn around. Nothing looked familiar. The backyards began to look creepier and creepier. All the muscles in my legs were arguing with my brain over walking another step. My legs were winning, but mission control was in complete disagreement.

Before my building fear turned into all-out panic, Joey spotted it. "Look. There it is!" Joey yelled.

Like two lost hikers finding their way back to the main trail, we hooped and hollered for joy. There it was, the top of the biggest chestnut tree in the city.

We were saved. The buddy system worked. Joey and I figured out how to get to school on our own. The fear I had envisioned of our pictures appearing on Wendt's Dairy milk cartons with the caption, "Have You Seen These Missing Kids?" immediately disappeared from my thoughts.

We had met the unknown and prevailed. In so doing, we went from the lowly rank of little kids to the higher tier status of kids, not requiring adult supervision at all times. Yes. We were on the road to big kid status.

With our new-found confidence and title promotion, our next challenge was how to make walking to school a lot more fun. One day, as Joey looked at the cracks in the sidewalk, he made one of his greatest observations.

"Hey, Fred. You know this stuff looks a lot like the cracks in the ice I saw at the Hyde Park pond last winter."

Shifting my lunch bag to my other hand, I quickly shot Joey an interesting question. "Is this the way to the North Pole?"

Not one to stifle a good make-believe game, Joey joined me in the new imaginary world I had just started, "The ice is cracking!" he shouted in fake terror.

I yelled back, "I'll save you, Joey! Hold on!"

And so it started. The daily search had begun to find the North Pole, headed by Admiral Freddy and Captain Joey of the Yukon, complete with polar bear sightings, ice rescues, and a lot of imaginary fun.

"It's a bad one! Watch out!"
"Better mark that one!" With chalk in hand, Joey dropped to the

concrete "ice" and began drawing an arrow with a skull and crossbones symbol and the word "DANGER!" on the badly cracked concrete section.

Whenever we found a construction company name stamped in the concrete, one of us would jump back, faking a close call. "A clue to get back home. Don't step on it."

By the time the school year was over, every section of every sidewalk had a warning sign plainly visible to all explorers who took that route. To add a touch of realism on cold winter days, I would toss the end of my scarf so Joey could grab hold of it.

With Joey clinging onto it with both hands, I'd reel him in, hand-over-hand, struggling and pulling hard on the scarf. It was more like a tug of war between just Joey and me.

The almost daily lifesaving dramatics took their toll. By the end of winter, my mom would wonder how another perfectly flat scarf could turn into a wet, twisted woolen rope.

Several weeks after our first solo trip, I saw something that caused a bit of alarm. Using my best ventriloquist skills, I quietly directed Joey's attention to my left, "Is that your Aunt Helen over there behind the big bush?" tilting my head in the direction that he needed to look.

Joey playfully twirled around like a ballerina and gave me the bad news, "Yup. that's her!"

We had been tailed all this time. Instantly, the exalted status of "fearless explorers" melted off us like Frosty the Snowman's last day in the sun. Right on that spot, Joey and I were busted back down to the rank of "little kindergarten kids." Even so, all those hours walking to school and playing, worked their magic. Joey and I would be best friends forever.

Right after Joey, came Bobby. Bobby was in our group because he could get us into his dad's church gym to play basketball on Saturday afternoons. Besides that, you could count on Bobby to wear his Cleveland Avenue School tee shirt to class every day.

Bobby insisted, "It's our school uniform. You are supposed to wear it." Since he was the only one we ever saw wearing the school's tee-shirt, no one believed him.

The best explanation for Bobby's school attire came from Joey. "Yeah. His mom makes him wear that shirt, so he doesn't forget it's a school day." A theory that held water since I never saw Bobby wear it on a Saturday or a Sunday.

To his mom's credit, Bobby did get a perfect attendance award for two years running. With all the colds I got in the winter, I would be lucky to set a perfect attendance record for even three weeks in a row. I'm pretty sure a tee shirt would not have helped my ability to show up to school, especially in December.

Bobby also had a reputation for being a bit of a prankster, relegating him to more than the average amount of time standing in the classroom punishment corner. The sight of

Bobby facing that corner helped the entire class understand the concept of stocks as a form of public punishment during colonial times.

Bobby didn't seem to mind the humiliation, though. He always seemed to be confident and content, planning his next prank for when he got back to his desk.

I heard that years after high school, Bobby went on to write self-help books with titles like *How to Use Your Time Wisely When Life Puts You in a Corner* and *Ten Muscle Strengthening Exercises While Standing Stock-still.* Turns out, being sent to the corner had its benefits.

Rounding out our foursome, with his unique no-part bowl-style haircut, was Rodney. Styled by his dad, it was an exact replica of the hairstyle that Moe wore on the comedy show *The Three Stooges.* Rodney's hair also had a stubborn cowlick that defiantly stuck out on the top of his head, rain or shine.

If nothing else, he had a really neat superpower.

Everybody knows that when it comes to neighborhood pickup games, it's hard to get the same number of players on each side. One team would always be one player short, but not in our neighborhood.

It turned out that Rodney possessed this uncanny knack for showing up all the time, rain or shine at the exact moment we needed to even up sides for any sport like kickball, basketball, dodgeball, baseball or badminton.

We had no idea what street Rodney lived on, or whether he had super hearing, or what. All we knew was that Rodney would show up, without fail, at just the right time, to even up the sides. Of course, his superpower had one weakness. He was always picked last.

I need to mention another thing about Rodney. He yawned a lot during the school day. Rodney had to get up very early every day to help his dad deliver milk from Wendt's Dairy to just about every house in the city before getting dropped off at school.

All the kids were envious over his riding in his dad's milk truck, except me. I valued my sleep and had to be dragged out of bed, get dressed, and forced to wolf down a bowl of cereal before being shoved out the door.

Even though it would take a collection of books as big as the *Encyclopaedia Britannica* to cover all the kids in my neighborhood, me, Joey, Bobby, and Rodney were typical of most kids in our town – unaware of the world events and always ready for the next day's worth of new adventures.

.

Chapter Two

If It's 1958, What Are You Doing Here?

The calendar on our
kitchen wall read 'January
1958' printed in bold letters
above a photo of a storefront
covered in snow, with an
advertisement for McGrath
and Durk Hardware Store
in bold typeface across the
bottom.

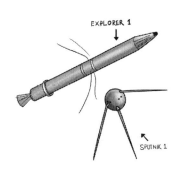

With my trusty black Crayola crayon, I scribbled, _Hurray for Explorer 1,_ circling it in red three times for attention. Looking at my artwork crammed into that tiny square reserved exclusively for the 31st day of January, I couldn't help but blurt out loud, "About time!"

I quickly looked around the room. The coast was clear. No one was around, not even my sneaky little brother Ronnie. I let out a sigh of relief. "Better not get caught talking to myself again."

Joey had warned me once, "If you keep talking to yourself, people will think you're bonkers."

"Talking to my toys don't count." I protested. That was undoubtedly true since Joey did it all the time.

Oops! I said it out loud again. Slapping one hand on my

mouth, I quickly looked around. No witnesses were anywhere in sight. *Whew! Nobody.*

News of America's pencil-shaped satellite was all over the radio, television, and newspapers. American ingenuity had finally prevailed and answered Russia's successful <u>*Sputnik 1*</u> shot into space.

I stared down at the *Niagara Falls Gazette* newspaper under my feet on the floor. The paper was too big for me to handle without all the pages falling out. It was a skill I had to learn someday, but for now, it made a nice floor mat.

The headline read, "*Explorer 1* Successfully Launched!" with a story under the banner saying that the United States was now in a good position to challenge the Russians in a race to see whose footprint would be photographed on the moon first.

Even though we were in second place right now, I imagined NASA would pull out all the stops and make it to the moon first for two simple reasons. First, if all the road signs on the moon were in Russian, it would be super easy for us to get lost, especially if there weren't any gas stations to ask for directions. Second, it would be hard to figure out how to get bottles of oxygen out of a Russian-made vending machine if the instructions were in all in Russian. We just had to get there first.

Even though the U.S. had finally figured out how to jump the gravitational fence separating us from the rest of the universe, for now, cheap tourist-class seats on a spaceship would be delayed a few more years. But surely before high school, a cool lunar exploration vacation would replace the Space Mountain ride on my wish list at Disneyland.

While I waited, all kinds of new gizmos began finding their way to department store shelves at a dizzying pace. Besides Silly Putty, decoder rings, stovetop popcorn, orange-flavored Tang, battery-operated toys Hula Hoops for the kids, adults marveled at the new no-stick frying pans, Chop-O-Matic vegetable chopper, hi-fi stereo record players, color television with big 20-inch diagonal TV screens and hundreds of other new gadgets.

My measure of technological progress had to do with cereal. The more toys hidden in cereal boxes, the more certain I was that we would get to the moon first. Along the way, I would learn that progress comes at a price.

One day, Ronnie decided to skip the before breakfast handwashing policy so he could beat me to the kitchen table. Spotting Ronnie's empty cereal bowl gave me some hope, but I had to act fast.

"Mom. Ronnie stuck his hand in the Frosted Flakes cereal box again."

"Did not," rang Ronnie's protest. "Did too," I objected.

"Did you wash your hands, young, man?" Mom was the one who enforced a strict before any meal handwashing rule, *especially* if you ate anything barehanded, cereal included.

Ronnie scowled back, "Aww, Mom."

"Off to the bathroom now."

With flakes of cereal stuck all the way up to his armpit, Ronnie pointed at my bowl and shot a squinty-eyed warning across the table. His message was clear. "One bowl at a time, or I'll tell Mom!"

As Ronnie disappeared down the hallway, Mom turned back to the sinkful of dishes. Grabbing the cereal box, I poured the rest of the contents into my bowl. With great anticipation, I watched for the toy to tumble out. By the time I stopped pouring, the cereal had already overfilled the bowl and was raining down onto the kitchen floor.

Turning the box towards me, I peeked in. There was nothing left in the box.

"Aww, shucks. No toy!" I grumbled out loud.

Mom whirled around, dishwashing suds splattering in every direction from her bright yellow rubber glove barely hanging on to her right hand. "What are you doing?"

Instead of apologizing, I blurted out, "No toy." Shaking the box to emphasize my point.

Her explanation came quick, ending with an apocalyptic warning. "It's in the trash. Next time, it's Cream of Wheat for you two boys!"

"But Mom. We don't like hot cereal in the morning!"

She replied, "It's not up to you to decide young man. Besides, after the commotion this morning, your dad will decide. And that's final."

Without asking, Mom launched into a blow by blow description of how the toy frogman somehow tumbled out into Dad's cereal bowl without notice, just as Dad's carpool buddies honked for him to hurry up. Trying to gulp down a few spoonfuls of cereal, Dad ended up chewing the frogman to pieces instead, causing a whole bunch of junk to transpire.

It was near complete pandemonium that morning, and now, if we were lucky, Dad would just switch to Cream of Wheat in the morning and leave Ronnie and me to search for toys hidden in every box of our favorite sugar-coated cereals.

"Is there another box, Mom?" Ronnie had finally returned to the kitchen.

My head snapped to attention, waiting for mom's reply. A new fight over cereal box mining rights was about to begin.

Chapter Three
"3-2-1-0 Blastoff!"

With all the rocket news
filling the newspapers, it was
easy to get excited about the
prospects of space travel. It
didn't take long before the kids
in my neighborhood came up
with the idea to start a rocket

club so we could pass all of our discoveries along to the new
U.S. space agency.

Normally we were usually too busy arguing over who was
the most powerful comic book hero to take any time to write
down rules for any kind of club. What we did write down was
that Joey liked Superman, and Rodney thought Flash was the
best of all the superhero comics.

Bobby loved Spiderman, probably because he could
climb walls with no problem, something Bobby, no doubt,
contemplated every time he found himself standing in the
corner. As for me, I was fascinated by Wonder Woman since
she was cool and looked a lot like my Mom.

You could bet the girls had all their club rules written
down in a three-ring notebook before they did anything else,
like arguing over who's doll was dressed the best. Guys were
different. Wired to build things from scratch and then knock
them to smithereens - just because. Cars and trucks ruled, so
making up club manuals would only distract us from the really

important stuff, like picking a cool club name or planning the next snowball fight.

"This meeting is hereby called to order," I announced with a no-nonsense voice of authority that I picked up from an episode of *The Little Rascals* TV show.

"First order of business is my buddy Joey has the floor, so listen up."

Joey stopped playing with his Buck Rogers decoder ring, stood at attention, and shouted, "Guys, we still need a name for our club." Heads nodded as club members took seats on my front porch steps facing Willow Avenue.

Joey took the first shot at it. "How about 'Space and Nothing Else'?"

"Hey. That spells SANE!" Richie interjected while pushing his broken glasses back up his nose. The center of his glasses sported a white wad of tape because of his run-in with a seventh-grader just the week before.

Even though we liked Richie, he had the lowest ranking in the club because he was at least one year younger than the rest of us. You had to be at least 10 years old to be taken seriously, even if you came up with great ideas most of the time. That said, Richie had paid all his dues, so we had to let him say his piece.

"So, what's the big deal?" retorted Joey to Richie's challenge on proposing SANE.

With a sideward glance at Joey, Bobby grinned and added, "Hey. Let's name our club 'Igloos Nutcrackers Space and Nothing Else'!"

"That's worse. That spells INSANE," countered Rodney with his freckled face contorted to look like he had lost his last marble, as he stifled a big yawn.

"Wait a second. I think Nutcracker is two words, so that spells INCSANE!" Rodney wasn't the best speller on our boys' team at school and usually was the first to sit down. If he lasted one round, that was a good day for him.

Bobby had ignored any need to explain why "Igloos" should be given a place in the new rocket club's name. Instead, he immediately fired back, "Is not!"

Rodney stepped closer to Bobby and yelled, "Is too!"

And so, another knock-down-drag-out verbal battle of "Is not! Is too!" had started.

An ear-splitting shouting match erupted, with everyone picking a side depending on who their closest friends were.

We were well into the twentieth round of the same two-word argument before I began pounding the porch stair with my baseball bat to get everyone's attention, "Order in the court. Order in the court!"

"Guys, guys!" Joey exclaimed excitedly, waving both arms for attention. "I vote we go with *Niagara All-Stars Rocket*

Association."

Barely keeping his glasses on his nose, Richie jumped up, "Or better yet, NARA for *Niagara Amateur Rocket Association!*"

Like deer in the headlights, Bobby and Rodney blinked and ceased advancing their unwinnable "Is too" and "Is not" positions. As fast as the argument had started, that is how quickly it stopped.

Joey jumped into the brief silence caused by Richie's amazing idea. "I nominate Fred to design a club patch with the letters NARA. All in favor?"

As each hand shot up in the air, Joey proclaimed, "It's unanimous."

After the meeting broke up, I protested to Joey, "You got me railroaded into this."

"Sorry," Joey said. "Votes are votes. You're it."

That weekend I sketched out a dark blue logo with a rocket and three orbiting atoms under the letters NARA and found an embroidery shop to make one patch for each member. It took all of the club's treasury, but they looked great. Building rockets would have to wait.

Almost a year later, we marveled as NASA revealed their

new logo to the world. There it was on page one of my dad's newspaper. My jaw dropped. There was no mistake. It looked a lot like ours. I immediately called up Joey dialing his home phone number, BU55490, as fast as I could. Within two minutes, Joey was at my house.

"Fred. How'd they see our patch?" Joey asked, staring at the newspaper story.

I held the paper in front of us like it was a letter declaring us joint winners of the Nobel Peace Prize in rocket science. "Easy. I bet the lady at the embroidery shop sent it to the President." Besides being that it was the only thing I could think of on short notice, it could very well be true.

"Wow. That's neato." Joey exclaimed.

At that moment, we felt proud that our club had made its first contribution to America's race to the moon. We couldn't wait to tell the other guys in our rocket club.

Chapter Four
Fizzy Powered Rocket Fuel

With our success helping NASA design their logo under our belts, the club turned its focus to building real rockets. With a little help from *The Mr. Wizard Show*, we were on our way.

Mr. Wizard demonstrated the gas-producing marvels of kitchen chemistry right before our TV watching eyes. Yes, sir. Mr. Wizard showed us how, by mixing vinegar and baking soda in a pop bottle, we could generate an invisible gas he called CO_2.

It didn't take much to figure out that by jamming corks into the bottle openings, the pressure inside the bottle would pop the corks like rockets high into the air. With cheap fizzy powered rocket power at our disposal, flights to the ceiling and beyond were now within our grasp.

I began covering all the corks I could find in aluminum foil attaching cardboard fins to make them look like the real thing. The guys in the rocket club would see how cheap and easy it would be to make corks fly like rockets. This was a huge scientific breakthrough.

At the very next meeting, I announced our first phase rocket building plan.

"Guys. We can make rockets by adding vinegar to baking soda and then quickly jamming a cork into these bottle tops." I handed out five bottles, corks, spoons, some baking soda, and then passed around my mom's bottle of vinegar.

It didn't take long. Within minutes, corks were popping from pop bottles in all directions. We were able to launch cork rocket after cork rocket, creating a stinky bubbling liquid mess on the porch steps in the process.

The technology spread like wildfire. All the kids in the club ran their own home experiments, that is until they were shut down due to a variety of mishaps.

Bobby and Danny were the first to have their test sites shut down, mostly for knocking over big bottles of vinegar. Bobby reported his incident in bitter detail, taking pains to underscore the dangers of mixing rocket fuel without taking proper safety measures, like screwing down the bottle cap before each launch.

My own rocket launching program came to an abrupt halt for a different reason. Ronnie and I ran out of vinegar from Mom's kitchen cabinet, a point we hoped wouldn't cause any real trouble.

I was minding my own business, just reading the latest edition of *Mad Magazine* in my bedroom, when I heard Mom call us. "Frederick! Ronald! Do you boys know where the vinegar bottle is?" My mom's exasperated tone of voice penetrated our closed bedroom door as if it wasn't even there.

Ronnie looked at me, figuring that I, as his older brother, would know how to reply. "Why no Mom. I don't know." I yelled through the closed door.

It was the truth, the whole unvarnished truth. Since I didn't know where we left the empty bottle, I really didn't know where it was now.

I could hear Mom's footsteps getting closer to the door. In a panic, Ronnie blurted out, "Rockets!" I quickly covered Ronnie's mouth to stifle any additional information he might feel compelled to offer.

Realizing my cover was blown, I stammered, "Yeah, Mom. Mr. Wizard uses vinegar and baking soda to launch rockets."

It was just a slight exaggeration of the facts. Ok, it was a big exaggeration, but Mom only watched the *I Love Lucy Show,* so she'd never know for sure.

The door to the bedroom opened in one swift motion, creating such a gust that it knocked two of Ronnie's finger paintings off the wall. Looking straight at me, Mom started off with a pointed question, "Did Mr. Wizard come to our house and take our bottle of vinegar? Where is it *exactly?*"

Taking my hand off of Ronnie's mouth and pretending to dust off his shoulder, I replied, "Not sure, Mom. Ronnie and me, well, sure we used some for our rocket experiments is all."

I hoped my reply struck the right balance between the cause of the problem and a good cover story to avoid punishment.

Besides, how could Mom punish her budding young version of Frederick the Great, boy inventor and his little brother Ronnie, even if we used all the vinegar in the house?

"You boys are both grounded." Mom was definitely mad."Go to Mr. Maroon's and buy a bottle. Now! Then both of you, back to your room until your father gets home."

So much for my "The TV made me do it" defense. At least once we got back from the store, Ronnie and I could quietly play in our room until our grounded sentence was either forgotten or we could work out a plea bargain at the dinner table with Dad.

Right now, we just needed to be on our best behavior, make the appropriate purchase at Mr. Maroon's store, and deliver our fresh shipment of rocket fuel supplies to Mom ASAP.

Chapter Five
Mr. Maroon Saves
The Day The Earth Stood Still

Hollywood had caught the science
fiction bug, literally, producing giant
insect movies like *Them* and creepy
films like *Forbidden Planet* and *Earth
vs. The Flying Saucers*. Joey and I
often found ourselves trying to figure
out how to round up enough money for each of us to cover
the twenty-five cent cost for a ticket. Sometimes we'd stand in
long lines for the matinee show, just to save a nickel.

On this Saturday morning, both Joey and I awoke, knowing
there were only hours left before the last showing in the city of
The Day the Earth Stood Still. We needed to take action before
it left town, possibly to never return again.

Wheeling my rusty old red toy wagon along Linwood
Avenue, I stopped at Joey's side door and called out, "Oh Joey,
oh Joey, can you come out and play?"

First, the inside door opened slowly. A second later, the
storm door flew open as Joey emerged wearing his Davy
Crockett raccoon hat and a lucky rabbit's foot on his belt. By
the looks of things, he was ready for action.

"So how much do we need, Fred?" Joey inquired as he
settled in next to me, anticipating my assessment of our
situation.

I looked down at the cigar box sitting on the floor of the wagon, locked securely with a strategically placed straight pin and a piece of electrical tape from my dad's workbench. I opened the lid and peeked in.

Carefully counting out the skimpy number of coins in the box, things couldn't be bleaker.

"We only need nine more cents before the movie starts," I said in my best matter-of-fact voice.

Joey thought for a minute, "OK. Before we start, I vote we make a pact." I nodded my approval.

By twisting our pinkies together and looking eyeball-to-eyeball, Joey said: "Repeat after me."

"One is as good as none."

I repeated, "One is as good as none."

Basically, we either saw the show together, or we both didn't go at all. One ticket was as good as no tickets. Our solemn oath pinky-sealed-promise was ironclad and irreversible. There was nothing left to do now but to resume the search and press on.

"Forward," Joey yelled, pointing up the street with the tail of his hat bobbing up and down as we marched along our usual route, looking for any and all pop bottles.

An hour later, Joey sighed. "Looks like *everybody's* got the same idea."

Trying to build up morale, I ponied up my best cowboy comeback: "Don't give up just yet pardner. Thar's gold in them thar hills."

My remark made Joey beam, "You right kemosabe! Two bottles behind you. Look now!"

I wasn't buying it. "Sure, there is. Right. You just want me to turn around and say 'April Fools.' So, ha, ha. No way."

"Boy Scout's honor. Turn around." Joey was insistent.

Figuring Joey had been referring to *The Lone Ranger and Tonto* TV program, I replied, "Tonto speak with forked tongue."

Joey sighed, "Suit yourself, cowboy." When I heard that, I knew Joey wasn't fooling.

On the ground behind me, were two empty glass pop bottles gleaming like diamonds in the dirt. With only an hour left before the show, it was time to warm up and cash in what we had so far.

"Ting! Ting!" rang the bell attached to the door as we entered Mr. Maroon's grocery store. Joey set the two bottles on the glass countertop next to the cash register. By our count, we were still a full nickel short. It was clear, only a small miracle could save the day.

Like an agent in the county assayer's office, Mr. Maroon appeared and set to work examining our meager haul for the all-important "Return for Deposit" lettering molded into the bottom edge of each glass bottle.

"Ok, boys. Looks like I owe you four cents. Here you go."

Joey replied glumly, "Thanks, Mr. Maroon. We'll be back soon, we hope."

No one was in the store, so Mr. Maroon continued. "If you don't mind me asking, what are you boys up to?"

Joey pleaded our case. "Uhh. Fred and me, well, we're trying to get exactly nine cents for two tickets to see an outer space movie at the Cataract."

When Joey was done, I added: "It starts in less than thirty minutes, Mr. Maroon."

Suddenly Mr. Maroon's eyes twinkled, and his thick mustache smiled back as he digested the details of our plight. "Oh, well, you've come to the right place, boys."

Looking up each sleeve and waving his hands like a magician, Mr. Maroon raised his index finger into the air. At the end of a slow, downward spiral loop, Mr. Maroon's finger hit the red "No Sale" key on the cash register. Like magic, the cash drawer popped open, with a loud ching-ching bell sound.

Reaching into the wide-open cash drawer, Mr. Maroon held up a bright shiny nickel for us to see. It wasn't just any nickel, it was a 1924 "S" (for San Francisco–minted) Buffalo Nickel, and it was going to buy us two tickets to the movies.

Handing the coin to Joey, Mr. Maroon gave us a few last words of advice, "Now run before you miss it."

I still remember looking at the nickel's shiny surface in thankful awe. With frenzied glee and a verbal flood of words, "Thank you, Mr. Maroon. Thank YOU!" we ran off and bought two tickets in the knick of time.

From our last row balcony seats, we watched as Klaatu's robot assistant, Gort, terrorized planet Earth with a menacing light-emitting helmet. We became science fiction movie fans for life that day thanks to Mr. Maroon's gift of a magical "no sale" nickel.

Years later, I found out that the nickel Mr. Maroon gave us was worth over $600, but seeing the movie when we did was worth more than all the gold in Fort Knox.

Story Four
Catastrophe in Mrs. Nelson's Class

Chapter One
Duck and Cover

My school made sure our classroom had all the latest state-of-the-art equipment. There was a <u>mimeograph</u> machine in the school office, specially designed room-darkening window shades to help us take naps, a basement Civil Defense shelter and a

ATOMIC BOMB TESTED DESK SHELTER MODEL 1A

phone linking each classroom to the principal's office.

But the most ingenious thing was our multi-purpose desks designed to secretly serve as personal protective bomb shelters in the event of an atomic bomb attack. They were so clever that any exchange student who came to visit would think it was just a desk, no secret to bring back to their own country to use. The ploy would have been perfect except for the fact that the inkwells never had any ink in them.

One day at school, I looked closely at the inkwell. Figuring Joey knew a lot of stuff, I waited for my chance to get his opinion. As Mrs. Nelson stepped out into the hallway to talk to the janitor, I saw my chance, "Hey Joey. Why don't we have ink in our inkwells?

"Cause girls got their pigtails stuck in them, and then boys got blamed for it getting ink on their dresses and all. That's why."

Unconvinced, I conjured up a second question, "Then why didn't Miss Williams just ban pigtails? That would have solved everything."

"Hmmm." The wheels in Joey's head were turning, "That's why they invented pencils instead."

That made a lot of sense since pencils didn't need any ink. Still, not filling the inkwells when exchange students showed up, was taking a big chance on national security.

Just then, Mrs. Nelson began walking back inside the classroom. Turning to look forward, I spotted one of Carolyn's pigtails dangling above my inkwell. A sudden urge washed over me. Yup! Dry inkwells were a boy's deliverance from doing time in the principal's office, and who knows what else. The temptation would have been overpowering.

A minute after returning to the classroom, Mrs. Nelson yelled out, "Duck and Cover. Duck and Cover. Get under your desks now!"

Surprised, we all dropped to the floor and sat under our desks, pulling our knees to our chins and covering our heads with both hands. It was a great comfort to know that our school desks would shield us from ceiling tiles that might be dislodged during an atom bomb blast.

After about five minutes, Mrs. Nelson called out, "All clear." Climbing out from under our desk shelters, I realized a pretty upsetting fact. It dawned on me that we didn't have school desks at our home for protection.

I didn't waste time. As soon as school was dismissed, I ran home and demanded an answer. "Mom? Why don't we have school desks at our house to protect us from air raids?"

"Don't be silly." came her unruffled reply. "You and your brother couldn't fit another thing in your room as it is, let alone a desk."

"But what if we get an atomic bomb attack?" I countered.

Not seeing the connection between desks and atomic bombs, Mom thought about it for a second. "Well, if we are all at home, we will just have to hide in the basement, of course."

"But, there are no school desks down there!"

Still not seeing my point, Mom responded in her no-nonsense, stop-being-ridiculous, tone of voice, "What makes you think you'd want to do school work in the basement during an atomic bomb attack?"

"But Mom, you see at school we all have ahh…."

Impatient, with my attempt to come up with a convincing explanation, Mom looked up at the ceiling, rolled her eyes, and cut me off in mid-sentence. "You can't bring your school desk home, and that's that."

Raising her index finger like a conductor signaling for silence before the start of a musical score, she made it final. "Don't even think about it. Got it? Go wash up for dinner. Now, please."

And so with that, I was left with one desperate hope. If there ever would be an atomic bomb attack, I prayed it would happen on a school day.

Besides having an adequate supply of bomb shelters camouflaged as desks, my school also came equipped with a stereo-sound movie projector.

Movies like *Bambi, Pinocchio, Snow White, Old Yeller, Davy Crockett-King of the Wild Frontier*, and other full-length Walt Disney movies would be shown in the gymnasium. The only thing about watching movies at school was that you had to sit on the hard wooden floor the entire time without popcorn, candy, or a fountain drink. Somehow, that all didn't matter.

The entire gym full of kids waited impatiently for the lights to be switched off as they stared up at the freestanding giant 72-inch silver screen on the stage. When the lights went off, we could see big numbers appear on the screen.

"Five, Four, Three, Two, One....!" the countdown ended in perfect unison from every voice in the jam-packed room: "Zero!"

As the ear-splitting sound came up, we kept our fingers crossed, hoping that the film wouldn't break for the next hour and a half.

The movie's flickering images were magical. Every movie drove home important life values, including dangers such as accepting and eating bright red apples offered by witches with funny black hats. We also learned to say "No!" to  drinking anything that bubbled or foamed out of an unlabeled clear glass bottle, or else who knew what would happen to you.

By the time I got to Mrs. Nelson's sixth-grade class at Cleveland Avenue Elementary School, I had seen every Disney movie. So it wasn't hard for me to match her up to Snow White in my mind. After all, she was pretty, pleasant to talk to, and had a soothing tone of voice that helped motivate all her students to do their best work. She also expected us to hand in each assignment on time, every time, with no excuses.

For one thing, unless you had proof of an alien spaceship abduction, or you had *Niagara Gazette* pictures showing you got stranded on an ice floe in the Niagara River, her attitude was, "Do or don't do, but never make an excuse for not turning in your assignments. If it's not finished, be honest and say so."

Mrs. Nelson told us that a good person does not lie or misrepresent the facts. Mrs. Nelson explained more than once about her greatest fear for us.

"Now class, when I'm retired, I don't want to see you on a televised congressional hearing saying, "Sorry, Congressman

Smith. You are correct, I learned how to lie in Mrs. Nelson's class."

"Raise your hand and promise me you will never do that." We took the pledge right there. "Yes, Mrs. Nelson."

Besides disappointing Mrs. Nelson, if you ever got caught telling a lie, you could count of being sent to the principal's office with a note giving the full extent of the charges against you. Most kids would rather walk a pirate ship's plank into shark-infested waters than pay a visit to Miss Williams' office for any reason.

Sometimes the classroom phone would ring, jangling the nerves of anyone that had been tardy or who might have been spotted running down the hallways that day. It was in those moments that promises of divinely inspired good deeds were made, in hopes of being spared the consequences of a personal audience with the principal.

Turning to face the class, Mrs. Nelson's gaze fell on the wrongdoer like a laser beam guided missile. "Jimmy."

"Here, Mrs. Nelson," Jimmy fessed up as all the boys sighed in relief, thankful their name wasn't called. For some reason, unlike the boys, it always seemed, the girls never flinched whenever the phone rang.

"Take this and report to the principal's office immediately."

As Jimmy trudged to the door, note in hand, a long drawn out "Oooooooooooooo!" emerged from every voice in the class.

Many of the promised good deeds had already been forgotten.

As the classroom door closed, notes and whispers circulated speculating on the possible infraction and the punishment that would be delivered by the school principal, Miss Williams.

It didn't take long to figure out how to stay out of trouble. The best course of action always was to stay in Mrs. Nelson's good graces by being on your best behavior and doing your best work.

As a reward, gold star stickers would appear on our papers, accompanied by a handwritten "Good job!" or "Keep up the good work!" message. That year, I sent both gold star papers to Santa as proof that I deserved every toy on my wishlist.

The best recognition of all came whenever Mrs. Nelson would assign someone the task of erasing the blackboards. This included tapping out the chalk dust from all the erasers right after school. There was nothing like the smell of chalk dust in the air and the pride of wearing a shirt spotted with chalk powder from Mrs. Nelson's blackboard.

For all the days in Mrs. Nelson's class, I only achieved that honor one time for doing an extra science report on jet airplanes.

"Mrs. Nelson?" I asked, still scrubbing the day's assignments on the blackboard.

"Yes, Fred" Looking up from her desk.

"Yeah, I want you to know, I'm going to write a cartoon strip someday for the Sunday comics or *Mad Magazine*, or my own newspaper."

"I'm sure it will be a very funny comic strip."

Encouraged, I spun out my dream even further. "Yeah. It'll be about my little brother Ronnie. He's in second grade, you know."

Her pleasant reply was simple enough, "Well, I hope to see him."

As soon as I got home, I told Ronnie to start practicing his blackboard erasing skills.

"What for?" asked Ronnie, figuring it sounded like work.

"You just gotta, that's why. Besides, Mrs. Nelson will be looking for you."

Even though Ronnie didn't understand my feeble attempt at explaining what a privilege it was to clean Mrs. Nelson's blackboard, for me, that memory would never be erased.

Chapter Two
The Assignment

A considerable amount of snow fell during the year we spent in Mrs. Nelson's class. Drifts had piled up higher and deeper until they reached the gutters on some of the houses on our street. After months of building snow forts, snow caves, snowmen, snow angels, sledding, and skating non-stop on our backyard ice rinks, Joey, Ronnie, and I began to wish for a quick end to winter.

It was right after the last snowman melted into a mound of slush that Mrs. Nelson called our class to order with news of a new project.

Giving the bottom edge of the world map a quick tug, the class watched the top tube effortlessly roll up all the continents, countries, islands, and cities of the world into a tight coil. As the map disappeared from view, everyone's eyes focused on the neatly printed words on the blackboard behind where North and South America once stood.

Smiling, Mrs. Nelson turned, picked up her wooden pointer, and began to explain. "Class. I have an exciting puppet show project for you all to work on over the next two weeks."

Without turning to look at the blackboard, the red tip of her pointer magically came to rest on each word exactly as she said them out loud:

"NEXT ASSIGNMENT

CLASS PUPPET PRESENTATION

DUE IN TWO WEEKS"

Grabbing a piece of chalk from the blackboard tray, Mrs. Nelson underlined the words DUE IN TWO WEEKS, adding an exclamation point to emphasize the deadline.

Wow! I thought. *Mrs. Nelson is the best. We have two whole weeks to work on a really neat project.*

In her nicest teacher voice, Mrs. Nelson continued. "Listen carefully as I assign each of you to a team. Each team will write an original story. By using puppets that you will build, your assigned team will act out the story for the entire class. The team with the best play will have the honor of performing it once more for the principal, Miss Williams."

I was good with everything she said up until the last part.

Joey was fiddling with the cover on his empty inkwell when I glanced over. Joey told me once that his left ear was missing a part, so he could only hear out of his right ear. Luckily my seat was on his good ear side.

"There you go. Another fly in the ointment." I whispered to Joey, shortly after hearing the principal's name.

Joey pushed his face down on the desk and looked sideways right at me. "Now that would have to be a pretty big can of ointment!" Joey grinned, as he whispered back.

"Who wants bugs in their ointment anyway? Certainly, not me." Joey laughed at my remark. We struggled to stifle our laughter, almost getting caught in the process. Like spotlights from a guardhouse heading in our direction, Mrs. Nelson's eyes washed over the classroom, looking for the source of the whispers. Joey and I immediately sat up, looking like marble statues sitting at our desks, holding our breaths, still trying to stifle the last telltale giggle.

Joey was right. The principal was way too big for any jar of ointment I ever saw, and for sure, she wasn't a fly or anything like that. I just hoped that if my team won, Mrs. Nelson would forget that last part altogether.

Grabbing a piece of paper from the top of her desk, Mrs. Nelson started calling out the members for each team: "Team 1: Rebecca, Shirley, Linda, and Robin."

Whew. I was sure glad I wasn't on Robin's team. She was always asking me to carry her books to and from school, like I had magical powers or something. It was all I could do to carry my violin, lunch bag, and my dad's leather WWII Army briefcase I used for a school bookbag.

Besides, there was no way a boy would ever do anything like that. At a minimum, you would end up playing catch by yourself for the rest of your life. I didn't see any point in worrying anyway. Robin wasn't on my team, so that crisis was never going to show up on my doorstep. Not ever.

I held my breath each time a new team was called. Before I knew it, there were exactly four kids still not on any team. Given the fact that there also were exactly four kids in Mrs. Nelson's class that ate, slept, and loved space adventure comic books, movies, and decoder rings, you might think it was blind luck that Joey, Bobby, Rodney, and I ended up assigned to the same team, but it happened.

Mrs. Nelson made it official. "Team 5: Joey, Freddy, Bobby, and Rodney."

There it was. Four classmate friends, belonging to the same rocket club, all on the same team. Looking back now, it seemed like a strange cosmic force was at work in Mrs. Nelson's class that particular day. I bet if we just looked harder, we might have seen the handwriting on the wall just above the blackboard, "Be warned. Laughter, pathos, and calamity will soon be at your door." In other words, in life's daily distribution of Chinese fortune cookies, we had just been handed a doozie.

For now, all the teams were in place, the table was set, the die was cast. We were destined to experience the hand of fate hiding behind a cloak of happy coincidence, winging its tried-and-true knuckleball straight at us. Peppered with a hefty dose of mayhem, it would teach us that lessons can be learned in embarrassing moments even when your favorite teacher, classmates, and principal are all present to witness a virtual kaleidoscope of gaffs and blunders.

At least for now, Team 5, was mercifully in the dark.

Chapter Three
Dust-to-Dust, Do or Bust

The weeks flew by like a Nike Ajax missile in hot pursuit of an enemy bomber. Mrs. Nelson's class assignment was due in only two days. Monday was the day of reckoning, and nothing short of divine intervention was going to stop it.

From the moment Mrs. Nelson announced the assignment, the only thing my team had done was to agree that the story would be about a frog king, two guards, and a spaceman traveling to a planet named Xenon in a faraway galaxy.

Like American Revolutionary War heroes getting ready for the battle of Bunker Hill, Joey, Bobby, Rodney, and I were on my parent's basement floor, throwing everything we had into the fight to avoid a humiliating loss in front of the entire class.

Looking around, I could see that Joey's extraterrestrial puppet appeared to be more like a smiling lizard than the intelligent-looking frog king that we envisioned for the play. I had to get it off my chest.

Squinting in Joey's direction, I nonchalantly blurted out my concern. "Hey, that's not how a frog king is supposed to look! Where's his crown and webbed feet? What kind of a frog is he supposed to be? He looks weird."

"Don't worry. Aunt Helen is going to help me finish

when I get home. Trust me!" Joey's reassurance wasn't a bit reassuring.

Looking over at Rodney and Bobby, it was obvious they were taking shortcuts too. Bobby had found two Christmas nutcracker soldiers in his brother's toy box that morning. Both he and Rodney were now in the process of adding eyehooks at each knee and shoulder. Even though the puppets looked nothing at all like guards from a hostile planet, I didn't say a word.

Of course, my puppet, Captain Carson, was the designated hero of the story. His white cotton cloth spacesuit was hand-stitched mostly with the help from my Nona. The suit fit perfectly over the jointly-owned Howdy Doody doll we had gotten at our last birthday party.

By adding silver boots, gloves, and a square cardboard helmet, Howdy changed from cowboy to space-boy in a matter of minutes. The lightning bolt on his chest signified strength, power, and intelligence, a tall order for a puppet to live up to.

By 3 p.m. all our marionettes were dangling in front of the empty six-foot-square wooden box that had once stored coal to heat the house in the wintertime. I remembered how much I missed going down to the basement to help my dad shovel coal into the firebox on cold winter nights in my bunny-eared pajamas, with sewn-in slipper feet.

Every time my dad slammed the firebox door closed, hot embers flew out like fireflies in the summer night. "Holy Rip!"

my dad would exclaim, chasing each ember and smothering it underfoot before they set the house on fire. Once my parents switched the furnace to oil fuel, that winter night ritual stopped, and the coal bin was never used again. That is until Rodney came up with a great idea.

"Hey, guys. Let's use the coal bin for practice!"

Not wasting a moment, the four of us dropped what we were doing and began scaling the walls. Joey got to the top first yelling "Geronimo!" just before jumping in. A cloud of coal dust rose from the sooty black floor at the spot where he landed. One by one, Bobby, Rodney, and I scaled the wall and tumbled in. Once inside, chaos reigned supreme.

"Hey, watch out! You tangled my puppet! Stop stepping on my foot! Not my foot, my puppet's foot! Hey, you poked me! Watch it! Move over! Well, excuse me!" During the whole time, the only useful thing we learned was how to untangle puppet strings without tripping over each other.

Thirty minutes later, we were covered from head to foot in coal dust. Bobby was the first to realize we were wasting too much time having fun. "Hey, guys. We still need to finish writing our play, or we'll be goners for sure on Monday!" Like four jack-in-the-boxes covered in coal dust, we jumped out of the bin, leaving our puppets hanging on the top rail.

Sitting in a circle, it didn't take long before creative ideas started flying, and nobody was taking notes. Using both hands near my mouth to amplify the sound, I yelled again, "GUYS!"

Everyone froze like statues, moving only their eyes to focus their gaze in my direction.

"Let's have a space commander named Captain Carson, land next to an outer space king's castle. Guards find him hiding behind a big green fern tree, and capture him. He begs the king for permission to leave the planet before his oxygen runs out. The king gets angry and says, 'You land on our planet without being invited, and you don't like our air? Guards! Take him to the dungeon!' Next, Captain Carson gets thrown into..."

Waving his hands frantically to stop, Bobby interrupted. "Wait. Unless we have a happy ending, Mrs. Nelson won't like it."

Taking no notice of Bobby's comments, Joey added another idea. "Hey, remember the episode when Buck Rogers had a sword fight on one of the planets? 'Planet X' I think it was. Wow. Buck Rogers almost didn't get away."

Rodney sprung to life, "Yeah. I remember! I stayed awake the whole time. Boy, that was some sword fight." We all watched Rodney for another one of his classic sleepy-eyed yawns. Instead, all we saw was an excited team member covered in coal dust, beaming from ear to ear.

Rodney was right. Based on the movies we had seen, sword fights were pretty common in outer space, but we needed the action to look more futuristic for any chance to win first place.

Just when it was about to get quiet, Bobby chirped, "I got it! Let's use aluminum foil to make weapons with a ball on top that shoots Zapper Rays."

As every team member shook their heads in approval, Joey piped in, "And why not have a big spitball fight to see who gets to fly the rocket from Earth?"

Rodney saw the flaw in Joey's plan. "Hey Joey. We don't have enough spaceman puppets!"

It was Bobby's turn again. "Maybe we could have the opening fight break out between Captain Carson and an invisible pirate. Besides, invisible stuff is everywhere you look in outer space."

"What kind of pie in the sky idea is that?" taunted Joey.

Bobby shot back. "Mockingbird pie is keen, if you know what I mean, jelly bean."

Listening to all the creative input swirling around, I yelled out at the top of my lungs, "Fellas! We have one puppet astronaut, and even he can't fit in our rocket ship."

"Details, details." Joey joined in waving his hand in the air as if a mosquito was buzzing overhead.

"And another thing." Rodney interrupted, "We need a coat of arms for the king's castle. A couple of frogs with tinfoil covered Zapper sticks should do it."

Not wanting to be out done in the idea department, Bobby jumped up, "How about using real frogs? I have one under my bed in a shoebox. I caught him in my backyard with my dad's fishing net and a flashlight. He's a beaut. We can get more at the Hyde Park pond and use them in our school play!"

The idea had merit since Joey's alien king looked like a cross between a frog and a lizard, or maybe a funny-looking toad if you squinted hard enough. These would be the real deal.

Bobby continued his frog argument. "For the finale, we can put ten frogs on stage after Captain Carson's rocket ship flies by the throne room window. Wow! That will be some action-packed ending!"

It sounded good, but I had no idea if it would actually work on stage, so I did what all good directors do. I promised whatever was needed to keep the crew happy. "OK, I'll ask Mrs. Nelson to see if she'll let us use real frogs, but only *IF* we win best play first. OK?"

I figured since our team needed to get past two all-girl teams, the chances were slim to none that I'd ever need to talk to Mrs. Nelson about Bobby's frog idea.With that idea settled, it was time to move on.

"OK, guys. Here's what we have so far. Captain Carson lands on Planet Xenon. Bobby and Rodney capture him. He goes in front of Joey's frog king. The king gives Captain Carson a giant sparkling gem as a souvenir from his visit and lets him take off back to Planet Earth. There will be three special effects, no sword fights, and nothing gets broken. We'll name the play *A Gem for Planet Earth*. Anything else?"

Joey shook his head. "Huh? Where did that come from?"

"What?" I shot back.

"The dumb title," Joey exclaimed with a grimace.

I pushed back in full defensive mode. "You got a better one?"

Joey scrunched up his nose as he spoke. "Yeah. What about *Frogs in Space* or *Diamonds on Planet Doom*. It was obvious. He really didn't like the title.

"Well guess what, I already told Mrs. Nelson." Staring back with both hands on my hips, I wasn't budging.

Just then, Bobby, Joey, and Rodney lifted their heads high, like deer trying to hear a faint noise in the forest. You could almost see their ears pointing to the doorway at the top of the basement stairs.

Bobby was the first to hear his mom. With a coal-smudged grimace, he announced, "Guys. I gotta go."

Everyone heard Joey's Aunt Helen calling, "Supper! Joey! Come home!"

111

Within seconds, Rodney declared, "I think my dad's calling." No one actually heard anything. I could see Rodney's hearing superpower was working, even in my basement.

Before anyone could move, Joey put up his hand and proclaimed, "All in favor of Fred finishing the script for the play say '*aye*.'"

Three "Ayes" came in quick succession. "Aye! Aye! Aye!" Even without my vote, it was unanimous. Feeling railroaded, I protested, "Hey! Why me?"

"Cause you named the play," Joey answered, "And because you have carbon paper is why!"

There was no arguing on both points. My dad brought home a whole bunch of carbon paper that my Uncle Dallas gave him from his job at Moore Business Forms. It was now up to me to finish writing the script, make three copies, lug the scenery to school, and have the special effects ready for the show by Monday morning.

One by one, Bobby, Rodney, and Joey made their exit, running up the cellar stairs and into the fading light of the day.

I could hear the guys outside yelling, "See you later, alligator. After a while, crocodile."

For their part, Bobby and Rodney would go off and wrap two cotton ear swabs in aluminum foil, making them look more like futuristic fly swatters than space-age swords. As for Joey, I crossed my fingers and hoped that Aunt Hellen knew what a frog looked like.

All alone in the basement, it dawned on me. We really did have a chance to win for best play honors over the entire class, and maybe, just maybe, Mrs. Nelson would forget to invite Miss Williams for a second performance. Since Mrs. Nelson never forgets anything, there was as much chance of finding a four-leaf clover in a snowstorm on the Fourth of July with your eyes closed for that to happen.

I just shook my head, not wanting to think about it any further, "Maybe second place wouldn't be so bad," I mumbled out loud.

"I heard you!" Joey had forgotten his puppet and returned to find it.

Trying to put on an air of confidence and squelch any display of fear, I took up the challenge. "There's no such thing as a runner-up trophy in a gunfight."

Joey ran up the cellar stairs, yelling back, "Say your prayers, hombre."

At a loss for a better cowboy comeback, I fired back with my best reply. "I reckon I'll be seeing y'all at the Sunday going-to-prayer meeting mañana."

It was a combination of something my favorite cowboy hero would say and something my mom and grandma taught me.

Prayers were always a good idea before doing anything big or important. Monday morning's play was big *and* important.

As Joey vanished out the door, I could hear my mom's voice filling the entire basement with her operatic voice, "Supper! Upstairs! Now!"

It was amazing how the second-floor clothes chute worked like a two-story-high bullhorn. "Yes, Mom. Be right up."

Taking two steps at a time, I bounded past my grandparents' first floor flat, running up two more flights of stairs before reaching the door leading to my parent's kitchen. Ronnie and Dad were already seated. Mom was putting a large bowl of pasta on the table just as I closed the hall door behind me. Dinner smelled delicious.

Tomorrow, I would say my best prayers at church, that somehow our play would be the best, even though we didn't have a script or had the time to practice our lines.

For now, everything seemed right with the world, and Monday was far away.

Chapter Four

Let the Puppet Shows Begin!

Except for the big puppet show
assignment, it was a typical Monday.
Joey and I were already having fun with
our puppets. I wiggled Captain Carson in
front of Joey's puppet, "Hey King! Klaatu
barada nikto."

Recognizing the lines from *The Day the
Earth Stood Still*, Joey responded, "OK.
Then no gems for you, Earthling." We both
giggled. "Uh, Fred? What the blazes does 'Klaatu barada nikto'
mean anyway?"

"Not a clue," I replied.

One thing for sure, whatever the woman actor said, it must
have been right or who knows what would have happened. One
mispronounced word and Gort could have served her an egg
salad sandwich from the spaceship's refrigerator or worse.

Besides that, while everyone else in the theater worried that
Gort might incinerate every creature on the planet, I was upset
that the taxi driver didn't get paid. The leading lady and Klaatu
left the taxicab and never once attempted to pay the driver.

It took days for me to finally realize that the cab driver
wasn't a real person, so he really wasn't harmed money-wise.
"It was just a movie!" I'd say to myself every time I recalled

that upsetting scene. It still didn't make me feel much better.

By the time Joey and I made it to Michigan Avenue, a bunch of neighborhood kids caught sight of my Captain Carson puppet.

"That's an astronaut? Really?"

"Where did you get a Howdy Doody spaceman?"

"Why does he have a box on his head?"

"Where is his oxygen tank?"

Joey and his puppet got bombarded with questions too.

"Is that a lizard or an alligator?"

"Why would a frog ever wear a crown?"

"Is it a magical toad?"

"Where're his warts?"

As we walked closer to the school, more kids with puppets appeared. There were doll puppets beautifully dressed in shiny cloth gowns, a doll that looked like a nurse, and a fairy book character that looked like a broken egg.

Wendy's tiger puppet, Cubby, looked cute and secure tucked halfway inside her school bag. It was fun watching his head bob up and down, arms flying in all directions as Wendy walked along the sidewalk.

Some of the boys' puppets looked like crew members from

Captain Hook's pirate ship, complete with eyepatches and clunky looking wooden swords. A few cowboy puppets, on stiff-legged horses, rounded out the collection.

The excitement was like a contagious wintertime cold, jumping from one kid to the next, before finally hitting a fever pitch just outside Mrs. Nelson's classroom door. Stepping into the room, we were met by an amazing sight.

First off, everything was rearranged in the room. The desks were pushed to one side to make space for what looked like a miniature stage. Attached above the front two legs on two yardsticks was a banner that read "Cleveland Avenue Elementary School Puppet Theater." The marquee glittered with shiny five-pointed stars.

Signs hung on each wall of the classroom announcing our plays:

"See it today! *Doubloon Island!* Watch as pirates find buried treasure in Jimmy's backyard!"

"Little Bo Peep Finds Her Lost Sheep in *Sheep are the Fuzziest Friends!*"

"Reflect on the wonders of *A Gem for Planet Earth!* It's Out of This World!"

"Watch as Cubby Tiger Goes to School in *Tigers Like to Spell Too!*"

"Don't Miss Seeing *A Rodeo Tail!* With Horses and Cowboys! Oh, My!"

Besides the signs, Mrs. Nelson had flipped over a large wooden table so that all four legs were sticking straight up in the air, like a bull that my favorite cowboy hero, Hopalong Cassidy, would have roped and tied to win a rodeo contest.

The paper backdrops for each play were fastened between the two back legs of the table. The puppeteers' legs would be hidden from view while the front side displayed the scenery for each play.

Looking closer, I thought, *This table looks familiar.* On closer inspection, I realized that this was the "gum table," the one my classmates used to ditch wads of bubble gum on as we made our way to our seats. Gum chewing in class was strictly prohibited, so any gum we forgot to throw away outside of school usually ended up stuck under this tabletop.

One time I accidentally dropped a pencil on the floor. I was a good five feet away, but like it was drawn by an invisible force, it slowly rolled all the way under the gum table. I noticed how muffled the classroom noises became the farther I moved under the table. Finally, reaching the pencil, I began backing up into the classroom. At the last second, I looked up!

In amazement, I gazed at a spectacular stalactite formation formed from years of gum deposited by students who came before me. The colors and textures formed by all those wads of gum made a masterpiece work of art. It was astounding.

A quick survey revealed that most elementary school kids preferred pink Bazooka brand bubble gum over any other flavor. Of course, that made me wonder why we never heard important information like this on any TV ad. "Nine out of ten dentists recommended Ipana toothpaste!"

So why not advertise this discovery also. "Scientific studies of classroom tables show that seven out of ten kids prefer Bazooka bubble gum over any other gum on the market. Buy some today."

I also suspected that all of the wads of gum came from the boy-half of the school population. Even without DNA testing, I was pretty sure I was right. I know for sure one of those giant pink wads was mine.

Where was all the gum now? Well, it seems Mrs. Nelson cleverly thumb tacked a large piece of Kraft paper to the underside of the table, fastening if all along the bottom frame to fabricate the stage floor. Once she flipped the table on its top, the paper stage floor hid it all. "Out of sight. Out of mind." I reassured myself. It was brilliant.

"OK, children. Team 1, you're up first." Mrs. Nelson announced in a cheerful voice.

As Team 1 got ready, I started to daydream, a subject that

119

would have landed me an "A" if it was graded as a classroom skill. Drifting off to memories of all that had happened leading up to our class assignment, I recalled our rocket club accomplishments, Mr. Maroon and the nickel, Nona helping with Captain Carson's spacesuit, the carbon paper copies of the script, and the fun we had in the coal bin playing with our puppets.

I was halfway through my morning daydreams when Mrs. Nelson called out, "Bobby, Rodney, Joey, and Fred, your team is next."

Chapter Five
Team 5, You're Up!

Holding our puppets and control sticks high off the ground, Joey, Bobby, Rodney, and I confidently walked to the back of the stage.

"Guys, don't forget to read your lines." Since we never had any time to practice, I slowly emphasized every word while handing out three smudged carbon copies of the script, giving Joey the first carbon copy because he was my best friend.

The paper curtain hid us as Joey and I flipped the background scenery showing Planet Xenon's rugged landscape. Once I placed Captain Carson behind the large fern tree that Joey had just taped down, we were ready.

The paper curtain rose. On my cue, Joey made rocket-landing noises as Bobby shook the table for realistic effect. Without any prompting, Rodney started dropping balls of cotton to simulate smoke coming from the rocket engine. It was all there in the script!

I looked over at Joey and whispered, "Joey. Land the rocket Now!"

"Oh yeah." Using the strings attached to each of the three rocket fins, Joey gently landed it on top of the "X" marked on the stage floor.

It was time for action. Bobby and Rodney grabbed their puppet control sticks and moved their nutcracker guards onto the stage. It was time for me to give the first line.

"I come in peace. Take me to your leader." Emerging from behind the fern, Captain Carson looked confident and unafraid.

With a swish of his silver fly-swatter-looking weapon, Rodney demanded, "You are in violation of Planet Xenon's laws forbidding you to land on our planet. You must follow us to the king of Xenon."

Captain Carson complied, "Take me to your leader immediately. I have a message from Planet Earth." Just like in the outer space movies, somehow all the people spoke English.

In a single file, Captain Carson followed the two nutcracker guards and marched off the stage.

The audience loved it.

We were like some kind of natural phenomenon. A well-designed car with zero miles on the odometer, and flying along at top speed, absorbing every bit of applause as our confidence grew.

As the applause died down, I quickly whispered, "OK, guys. Set up the throne room scene."

Rodney and Bobby flipped over the throne room backdrop, complete with its special effects window. The window revealed a skyline with flying cars outfitted with laser cannons, glittery hubcaps, and hood-mounted rockets. Rush-hour driving on Planet Xenon was like any other rush hour on any other planet - frantic and unfriendly. With Joey's frog king on the throne, we were ready for Act 2.

As the curtain rose, Captain Carson and the two palace guards marched in from stage left, stopping in front of the throne. Joey's king sat in tranquil calmness, looking at the captive with a friendly smile on his face. Joey's Aunt Helen had pulled it off!

"Great King of Xenon. We found this Earthling hiding on the palace grounds."

Given the circumstances he was in, Captain Carson knew enough not to get into any kind of 'Our planet is better than your planet' argument. "Your majesty, I come in peace from a beautiful planet called Earth, with lots of water and much smaller fern plants. Really, nothing like the great fern trees you have on your planet."

Revealing facts about Earth's abundant water supplies was probably not a smart piece of information to pass around to inhabitants of a dry, desolate planet with only fern trees for vegetation. Hopefully, the reference to small-sized ferns would make them lose interest in visiting Earth any time soon.

Captain Carson went on, "King, if you release me, I will

bring back all of Earth's important scientific discoveries to promote peace and prosperity between our two planets."

The frog king tilted his head up and down in agreement, "You may go, and as a token of our goodwill, please accept a gift to bring to your king."

Joey moved the frog king to the open treasure box announcing, in a good froggy sounding voice, "You may have any gem you wish as a gift for your planet."

Bowing Captain Carson, I replied, "Thank you, king!" That was the easy part. The next move had never been tested, even though it was key to the play's success. Captain Carson's part called for him to use his specially prepared glue-covered glove to make contact with a papier-mache gemstone in the treasure box and pull it out.

Holding the control string for Captain Carson's right arm, I moved his hand high into the air, dropping it into the treasure box like a move from a kung fu movie. Looking down, all the members of Team 5 breathed a sigh of relief. The gemstone prop sat nestled securely in the palm of Captain Carson's gloved hand. We were all smiles.

Lifting the glittering gem into view, the King of Xenon praised the Earthling's selection. "You are wise to have chosen our biggest jewel. Now go."

With words of praise and appreciation, "Thank you, King of Xenon," I moved Captain Carson off the stage as the large gemstone for planet Earth glittered brightly in the sunlight streaming through the windows from stage left. It was picture-perfect.

With Captain Carson out of view, Rodney and Bobby handed their control sticks to Joey and me before positioning themselves on each side of the throne room's back wall. Finding the ends of the special effects string, they crouched down, waiting for my signal.

"3...2...1....0!" Joey counted down as Bobby pulled, and Rodney let out slack, slowly moving the cardboard replica of the *U.S.S. Destiny 1* from behind the wall into the light of the cutout throne room window. Bobby pulled the cardboard replica into view, moving it past the window opening before making it disappear again behind the throne room backdrop.

It was perfect!

Joey's frog king gave the final line. "They have successfully left us in peace. Let us all be merry and begin the royal hopping festival."

The curtain dropped to boisterous applause and Mrs. Nelson's accolades. "Good job, Team 5. Good job!"

It was over. Miraculously we had pulled it off. No one could say the play was a bust. All this was even more amazing since my team never had time to do a dress rehearsal.

All I could think of was, *Prayers work!*

Chapter Six
The Bee That Spelled Trouble with a Capital T

Within minutes of the last presentation, Mrs. Nelson called for the class to quiet down. "Class, you all did a superb job on all your plays." She went on to say, "After a lot of thought, I have chosen Team 5 for performing the first-ever science fiction space adventure presented at Cleveland Avenue Elementary School!"

I couldn't believe my ears. We had beaten two all-girl teams; one team with two boys and two girls and one other all-boy team on our path to success. Given the history of our class, this was an amazing day.

As the sound of victory rattled around in my head, I pondered one question. If all the plays were that great, why did Mrs. Nelson really want our team to showcase our class assignment to the principal? Granted, we had the only science fiction play, but Wendy's team did a great job on their fairy tale about a tiger who loved to spell the name of every animal that was invited for dinner. Besides that, Robin's team had great scenery and an all-girl cast of puppets that looked real.

It was a known fact that the boys in my class never won a school contest against an all-girls team, but for some reason, Mrs. Nelson picked us! Maybe, I thought, we were chosen to build up self-confidence amongst the boys in her class? Maybe Mrs. Nelson felt guilty, and so this was a way to even the score a bit? Now that made sense!

Since recorded history at Cleveland Avenue Elementary School, *never* had an all-boy team won any of Mrs. Nelson's Friday afternoon spelling contests. Each week, the boys' teams would suffer humiliating defeats against a well-prepared all-girl team - sometimes with not one girl missing any words, as every boy sat at their desks, embarrassed but unconcerned.

Still, the closest any all-boy team ever came to claiming victory happened the time yours truly went toe-to-toe against two girls in the final rounds. At that moment, all I needed was to out-spell Wendy and Rebecca for the win, and the all-important "Nyah, nyah" bragging rights would be ours!

I was already picturing Mrs. Nelson's <u>fountain pen</u> scribbling '<u>*Boys Win*</u>' in the school's book of world records.

"Fred." Your next word is *collar*." As if I needed more information, Mrs. Nelson added, "A *collar* is found on clothing."

My mind spun into hyperdrive, *This is too easy. Something is up. I just had to spell orangutan for crying out loud. Was this one of those trick words with two different spellings?*

Why did she say, "On clothing?" Was it spelled differently if it was on a girl's dress? I only had a brother, so how would I ever know?

I shook my head and reminded myself that sometimes, too much thinking is not always a good thing. That's when it hit me.

Mrs. Nelson is a girl – she's on their side!!!

My once rock-solid confidence crumbled into a pail of sun-soaked beach sand. Seconds ticked by. I could feel beads of sweat forming on my hands and on the back of my neck as a chorus of voices in my head rang out a frenzied warning, "Collar has two *l*'s!" "TWO *l*'s!" The last caution came with sound advice and a strong warning, "Trust your first guess. Don't blow it!"

As I looked out, I could see the guys on the edge of their seats, holding their collective breaths. Their silent prayers were plastered on their lips, "Please, please, please, pretty pleeeease!" You know the usual stuff people say and do in a desperate attempt to somehow affect the outcome of a key game.

Watching the guys pulling for a home team victory, I felt like the mighty *Casey at the Bat* playing for the Mudville team. Only this time, I thought, *The home team is going to win!*

Confidently I squinted at a spot on the far classroom wall as the voice in my head carefully slow-pitched each letter, and the muscles in my voice box formed the exact pattern to belt them out of the park.

"C," my inner voice said.

"C," carefully moving my lips to form the sound, I said it aloud.

"O" ... "O"

"L" ... "L"

There was no stopping this slugger now. I already knew that the next letter across the plate was the same as the last. I took a breath, and without waiting, I called out the last two letters, "A" ... "R"...!

The moment hung in the air like the last note in an unfinished symphony.

In my overconfident impatience, a temporary brain-to-mouth communications breakdown had taken over. Once again, I knew that thinking something is not the same thing as saying it.

Mrs. Nelson gave her official call for all to hear. "That's incorrect."

My time at bat was done. I had struck out.

In a blink, all the male inhabitants of Mudville collectively gasped and slid so low in their seats they were nearly invisible. That day, the boys found another use for their desk-shaped atomic bomb shelters.

Mortified, I trudged back to my desk. Having come so close to breaking the girl-dominated spelling bee monopoly and also losing the all-important "Nyah, nyah. Haha, we won." bragging rights for the guys. For sure, my name was going to be mud around the playground for at least a week.

Right now, those spelling bee losses were as good as forgotten like all the obscure words in Webster's Dictionary. This was a new day. Spelling bees may be the field for the girls half of the world, but writing, producing, and performing plays was definitely one domain where boys could shine too.

"Come up front and take a bow, boys, and bring your puppets if you have them." Mrs. Nelson announced.

Standing in a line, I could see Rodney stifling a yawn as Joey whispered to Bobby, "We're number one. We're number one!" Joey was right. We had beaten the all-girl teams fair and square, and we were on our way to cap our boys' team victory with the next performance of *A Gem for Planet Earth*.

When you are unaccustomed to winning first place, the immediate feeling of pure joy can get squashed by the thought that you might be in over your head. So, like an anchor pitched over the side of a powerboat just a hundred yards from the finish line, it hit me hard.

Next performance? Oh my! A voice in my head sounded the alarm.

We had only cleared the first hurdle of a two-part race. To claim ultimate victory, Team 5 had to scale one last big mountain. We'd need to pull off another near-flawless performance in front of Miss Williams, the school principal, Mrs. Nelson, and a classroom full of classmates.

Shaking off any lingering doubt, a voice in my head shouted, "You'll do great. It's payback for all the humiliating spelling bee defeats. Bye! Bye! So sorry! Get ready to celebrate a really big win."

In the typical underdog's path to glory, pride had taken over control, completely squelching any thoughts of failure. It was all I could do to refrain from thumping my chest and letting out a Tarzan yell, "Aaaaah-ah-ah-ah-aaaah-ah-ah-ah-aaaah!"

Mrs. Nelson made it official. "Great job, boys. Wonderful play. Remember that Miss Williams will be in our classroom to see you do it again next week, Monday morning. Be ready. Take your seats, please."

There was no turning back now. My buddies on Team 5 and I were about to learn that the fall that comes after pride is not a season of the year.

Chapter Seven
Before the Fall

"Frederick. Ronald. Get up now, or you'll be late for school! Frederick. Don't forget your puppet. Hurry!" My mom's opera star soprano voice jolted us awake. The big day for the second performance of our winning play, *A Gem for Planet Earth,* was here.

By the time I finished breakfast, Joey was already at the side door, "Oh Freddy! Oh, Freddy!"

Emerging from the door next to the chain-link fence entwined with vines full of flowering morning glories, I could see that Joey looked worried. "We are going to be late. Hey. Where's your brother?"

Pulling the leather briefcase I used for a bookbag off the sidewalk, I replied, "Ronnie is going to see the dentist. Glad it's not me."

Holding his mouth wide open, Joey bragged, "Look. Dr. Zak said I didn't have any cavities. See!"

Quickly glancing at Joey's freckled nose and his wide-open mouth, I laughed. "Do you have Froggy in there?" Joey had nicknamed his puppet, Froggy, even though it still didn't look anything like a real frog.

Joey shook his head. "Nah. I left him at school so I wouldn't forget. The last one to school is a rotten egg."

Placing his foot on an imaginary starting line on the ground, Joey crouched down low to get a good start.

It was always a hassle carrying everything to school, and this time, I also had my puppet to carry. Shifting the violin case and briefcase to my right hand, I held Captain Carson straight out in front of me in my left hand.

"Ready! Set! Go!"

Rounding the end of the first block, Joey was in the lead. As Joey tripped over a big crack in the sidewalk, I saw my chance and dashed in front of him. Separated by inches, the race lead went back and forth as we jumped over sections of the sidewalk with big 'Danger' signs in chalk. One block from the school, it was anybody's race.

"Morning, Officer Casey!" Joey sang out to the school crossing guard as he waved us across Cleveland Avenue.

"Better hurry." Officer Casey warned us, just as the school bell began to ring. It was going to be a photo finish.

"Coming through!" Joey bellowed as he bounded up the three outside steps that led to the school doorway. "Beat ya this time, Freddo."

"I dare you to race me home." I replied, adding, "Double or nothing." Since I wasn't sure what was going to be doubled, I thought "nothing" was a safe bet.

"Deal," Joey responded with all the humility of a conquering hero.

Once in the classroom, we could see everything was ready. On the blackboard behind the stage, Mrs. Nelson had written, *A Gem for Planet Earth* under the heading "Today's Activities."

"OK, class. The principal will be here any minute. Remember to sit quietly until she gets here."

As if she was listening for her cue in the hallway, Miss Williams entered the classroom with a rush of excitement, like a celebrity on an opening night premiere.

"Good morning, class."

"Good morning, Miss Williams," the class replied in unison with polite smiles painted on every face.

Miss Williams took her seat in front, as the whole class found a spot on the floor and sat at attention around her. It was plain to see that Miss Williams was having trouble sitting in the uncomfortable baby bear-sized chair. Even Goldilocks would have skipped sitting in it during her visit to the three bears' house. Miraculously, the chair held together.

Seeing Miss Williams two feet away from the stage, I gulped hard, trying to calm my nerves.

All us kids knew that Miss Williams was pleasant enough whenever your mom and dad were around, but if you were told to go to her office, heaven help you! If you were caught breaking any of the long laundry lists of school rules, she was judge, jury, and jailor. There were no plea bargains. Any punishment she handed down would be relayed to our parents, who would add another level of retribution on top of it all.

Luckily, I had escaped Miss Williams' ire up to now. *Why worry?* I thought, *After all, we were the best of the best. What could possibly go wrong?*

Chapter Eight
Can the Principal Fire Us?

With just minutes to go before the curtain went up, Rodney stammered, "Sorry, Freddo. I left my puppet on my dad's truck. But I can get it tomorrow!"

As I stood there speechless, Joey quickly added, "Oh! Gee whiz! I forgot my script!"

Seeing an opportunity to unload his own bombshell, Bobby sheepishly added, "Didn't know dogs liked the smell of <u>carbon paper</u>. So hope you got extras."

Hitting my forehead with my free hand in full Director's panic, I yelled-whispered as quietly as I could, "How could you guys forget? I hope you memorized your lines!" Looking at Joey, Bobby and Rodney staring everywhere except at me, I knew they hadn't. Team 5 was in big trouble.

Fortunately, at that very moment, Mrs. Nelson was describing the puppet show contes and performances to Miss Williams. Everyone was totally unaware of our predicament. We had only seconds to think up something fast.

Just as my heart skipped another beat, I spotted Wendy

sitting a few feet away, holding her tiger puppet, the star of her play, *Tigers Like to Spell Too!*

"Hey, Wendy. Can I borrow your puppet?" Defensively placing her tiger puppet behind her back, Wendy took on a distrustful stance. It was the kind of body language that signaled tough negotiations were ahead.

"Uh, Wendy. You know, I could carry your books home from school. So, could I borrow your puppet right now? I mean, you know? Could I?"

Surprised by my unexpected offer, Wendy thought a moment and began to hand "Cubby" to me. The tiger was inches away from my grasp when it dawned on Wendy that she held all the cards. Smiling, Wendy replied, "Sure, only if you help carry my books *all* week."

The countdown clock was ticking. Mrs. Nelson would tell us to start at any moment. I shrugged and accepted. "Got it. OK. Don't worry. Trust me!" Hoping all the while that none of Wendy's girlfriends overheard our agreement.

Grabbing the tiger, I ran behind the stage. "Guys! We need something for his paw!" Joey and Rodney knew immediately what to do. Rodney pulled out a used popsicle stick from his pocket. While Rodney held it in place, Bobby taped it to the tiger's right paw. "There!" exclaimed Bobby as we looked at his handiwork.

The popsicle sword was fine but Cubby's sewn-on smile was not scary at all. It was more like a cute smile. "What are we going to do with the dumb smile? Rodney asked, not wanting a wimpy looking palace guard for his puppet.

"No one will notice. It's a tiger remember. Tigers are ferocious. Even cute ones! "

"You sure?" Rodney wasn't convinced.

"Yes!" I shook my head violently for emphasis.

"OK then," came Rodney's unconvinced reply.

With one big catastrophe averted, I whispered, "We still need a script!"

Just as Mrs. Nelson was finishing her story of how Team 5 had won the contest, I opened a leather flap on my briefcase and spotted a bunch of papers stuck to the bottom.

"The script!" Joey mumbled, while tossing his head skyward in pure joy over our newly discovered pardon from total disaster.

Bobby faked wiping his forehead. "Whew. Saved!"

Rodney yawned, covering his mouth before commenting, "That was close."

I let out a sigh of relief, "OK, guys. We can do this. Get ready for the curtain."

"Are you boys ready back there?" Mrs. Nelson's voice seemed a little bit anxious.

"Yes, Mrs. Nelson," I replied. "We are now."

Within seconds, two helpers from the class flipped up the paper curtain to reveal the rugged landscape of Planet Xenon. It was a hostile looking place with jagged mountains, rocks, and giant green fern trees.

The now famous red, white, and blue "Made in Japan" *U.S.S. Destiny 1* toy rocket began its descent to the stage floor. Realizing that the principal was in the audience, Rodney began to nervously shower the stage with cotton balls. Instead of rocket exhaust, it looked like a lake-effect blizzard had hit the landing site. Running out of cotton halfway through the landing, Rodney shrugged, letting out a muffled "Ooops."

Undaunted, Joey slowly guided the toy rocket to its touchdown on the stage floor, accompanied by an amplified version of loud rocket landing noises.

Except for Rodney's curtailed snowmaking efforts, everything was going fairly well, just like the first show. In fact, the opening seconds were accompanied by enthusiastic applause led by Miss Williams! Team 5 was all smiles.

A split-second before touchdown, a control string on one of the rocket landing fins broke free. The principal, Mrs. Nelson, and the entire class watched as the sharp plastic tip of the nose cone flipped down, tearing a large gaping hole in the stage floor! A second later, the entire upper section of the rocket sank below the torn paper floor as our classmates all cheered and laughed!

Without skipping a beat, Joey raised his voice, hollering out loud rocket crashing noises to match the action taking place on the stage floor.

In shock, I looked down to assess the damage. The rocket was definitely lost but Captain Carson was still hidden behind the fern tree. By luck, the rocket had missed him.

I whispered. "Guys. We can work around this. Keep going."

My whispers to press on suddenly turned into a chorus of loud muffled voices as a fight over possession of the lone script broke out!

"Give it to me! I'm next! Give me my line!"

In desperation, Joey elbowed Bobby to get his puppet onto the stage. Surprised, Bobby accidentally dropped his nutcracker soldier straight down. Suspended in mid-air, half free and half tangled in control strings, the guard appeared to be caught in a giant spider's web just inches above the stage floor. Bobby struggled to regain control.

Unaware of the commotion to his left, Rodney dragged his newly acquired tiger puppet into view. With lurching motions, first standing, then bent over, then to a kneeling position, and back to a precarious wobbly standing position, the tiger finally made his way to where Captain Carson was hiding.

Bobby's puppet, still hopelessly tangled and suspended a full foot above the stage floor, decided to demand that the astronaut come out and surrender immediately. "Attention! Intruder! Come out now. We have you surrounded!" Those lines were nowhere in the original script.

Rodney continued to add growls and menacing popsicle stick sword movements to make Bobby's point. Just before it was time to pop Captain Carson out from behind the fern, the tree toppled into the hole formed by the crash, disappearing completely from sight.

With audience laughter building and with the script nowhere in sight, I made up the best response I could think of. "I give up! OK? Please! I can explain!"

The audience broke a new classroom laughter record at

the new spectacle before them. This was not what they had witnessed during the competition for the best play and certainly not what a fearless spaceman would ever say.

"Follow us to our king now," Rodney commanded, ending his line with a long menacing growl.

With everyone in the audience in an uproar, the curtain closed on Act 1. I looked at my team. Joey and Bobby were red-faced, with Joey's freckles even more noticeable than usual. True to form, Rodney just yawned and rubbed his eyes, wishing he had stayed on his dad's milk truck that morning.

As the blood rushed back into my head, pushing back the fainting spell that had tried to take hold, Mrs. Nelson began shushing the class for quiet. Before another calamity could materialize, I gave the order. "Guys, the throne room scene. Set it up!"

When the curtain rose again, the aluminum-foiled throne, the king, and a big treasure box stood in the center of the stage just inches away from the gaping hole in the stage floor.

Even with most of the stage floor intact, the guards and Captain Carson all had to take different routes to get to the king. Rodney's guard marched in from stage left. Still hopelessly tangled up, Bobby had no choice but to enter his guard from the ceiling. Captain Carson strolled into view, completely unescorted, from stage right.

It was now Rodney's turn to talk, but since there was no way for Rodney to move the tiger's unfamiliar control sticks, hold the script, and recite everything at the same time, it was now up to me to hold the script steady for him to read.

Rodney squinted in my direction. "Your Highness, we caught this guy in our royal flowerbeds, snooping around." Pleased with his fictitious narration, Rodney shot a triumphant grin.

I glared back at Rodney, mouthing the words so he could see them clearly, "That's not your line."

Seeing my disapproval, Rodney whispered, "Your thumb is on my line." Sure enough, it was. Laughter spilled across the stage and up the backdrop, helping our hotter than normal ears get even hotter. The audience could hear everything we said!

With Rodney's speaking part done, it was now the king's turn to speak. Joey looked at me with panic written all over his

face. He had no idea what he was supposed to say. Joey needed to get his hands on the script like *NOW!*

Joey immediately reached across Bobby, as Rodney ducked just in time to let Joey grab the script from my outstretched hand. Unfortunately, the movement caused Joey to drop his main control stick. Kerplunk! Froggy dropped off his throne and into the hole in the stage floor.

Realizing what just happened, Joey began pulling up his control strings, but no amount of tugging could free the king. His frog foot had lodged on a giant wad of freshly planted Bazooka bubble gum, exactly where I had planted it a week earlier!

Seeing what was happening, Rebecca leaned forward from her front-row floor seat and reached in to help. Placing one hand on the king and her other hand on the stage's paper floor, she leaned forward. Without warning, the paper floor ripped, taking the treasure box, footstool, and fern tree to the bottom of the tabletop below.

Any pretense that the puppets were extraterrestrial creatures was gone. It was time to act. Immediately, four arms dropped into view, scurrying around the stage like sock puppets performing a pantomime skit.

Within seconds, the throne, the king with his now gooey pink webbed foot, and royal fern tree were back on what little stage floor was still intact!

Peeking around the corner of the marquee banner, I could

see a visibly upset Mrs. Nelson. To make matters worse, a distinctly perplexed principal looked at all that had happened, wondering how we ever got chosen for best play. With all the laughter, I hoped she might think we won for best outer space comedy.

At fifty decibels louder than usual, Mrs. Nelson's warning came loud and clear. " Class! Settle down now!"

As the commotion subsided, my team did the only thing we could. We pushed forward.

It was Captain Carson's turn to speak.

"King. Release me, and as a sign of peace, my planet will give you all the spaceships you need to conquer the galaxy." An offer, which besides not being in the script, did not make a lot of good intergalactic common sense.

Joey motioned with his frog's right hand towards the treasure box, still half-hidden below the stage floor. "Deal," Joey exclaimed. "Help yourself."

Taking no chances, I raised Captain Carson's arms high above his head. Diving headfirst, Captain Carson ended up flat on the stage floor, missing the gem by a good quarter of an inch.

Rather than trying to pick out a precious gem to take back to Earth, it appeared as if Captain Carson was trying to fix a drainpipe under the throne room floor as a goodwill gesture before he left for Planet Earth. The effort paid off, Captain

Carson's glove stuck to the gem!

With the glittering papier-mache gemstone stuck to his glove, Captain Carson returned to a standing position. "Thank you, King of Xenon. Goodbye, for now. I shall return with your ships."

As Captain Carson strode confidently out of sight, Bobby and Rodney took up their positions on each side of the throne room wall. It looked like our glittering gemstone, and final flyby special effects were about to save the play.

With Bobby and Rodney holding the ends of the string for the rocket flyby, I counted down, "3...2...1...0." Joey's loud rocket engine ds began to echo in the classroom. The audience watched the final scene with great anticipation.

As the cardboard rocket made its way across the window, Joey's frog king exclaimed, "They have successfully left us alone. Let us celebrate with a Hi-Yo Silver. Away!"

I shot Joey, my best disapproving frown, "What was that supposed to mean?" Joey just shrugged.

At that moment, another round of unfortunate events began to unfold. As Bobby and Rodney attempted to control the rocket string for the final flyby, the nose of the cardboard rocket caught the edge of the cut-out window frame just as it was about to disappear from view on the other side of the window cutout.

Hopelessly wedged, the rocket's motion came to an abrupt stop. A seesaw battle began as Bobby and Rodney started a series of tugs and pulls designed to free the rocket and string. In one last desperate pull, Bobby yanked as hard as he could.

Everyone watched as Bobby and Rodney slid across the polished classroom floor in opposite directions, with pieces of the window frame, cardboard rocket, string, and throne room wall all in hot pursuit. Joey and I stood like shocked statues, overcome by a new level of embarrassment. It was as bad as if we had forgotten to button up our trousers after visiting the boy's lavatory.

That was all the audience could take. Kids jumped up and pointed at the demolished stage, each talking excitedly to their nearest neighbor on what they had just seen.

After all, they had just witnessed the best special effects surprise endings they would ever witness during a puppet show in their entire lives.

As if we needed a critic, Joey's frog king appeared to be looking up at us, shaking his head in total disbelief. Whatever chance Team 5 had of salvaging a victory for all the boys in Mrs. Nelson's class, was now gone.

"Oh, my!" Miss Williams declared. Without saying another word, she stood up and left the classroom. Mrs. Nelson ordered everyone to get to their desks and put their heads down. That meant Team 5 too.

With everyone's head down on their desks, things got quiet, pretty fast. Except for a faint muffled croaking noise, you could have heard a pin drop. That's when it happened.

The girls closest to the cloakroom door began screeching and running to Mrs. Nelson, as four huge frogs leaped between the desks on their way to the door leading to the hallway in hot pursuit of Miss Williams!

Miss William's screams assured us that besides our disaster of a play, she didn't much like frogs either. The uneven sound of one shoe and then one stocking foot hitting the hallway floor confirmed she had lost a shoe on her dash for safety. A split second later, all four frogs caught up, jumping back and forth as Miss Williams peered horrified through the office door window, still struggling to catch her breath.

Wide-eyed and shaking, Mrs. Nelson gave the orders, "Boys! Pleeease get those out of the school! NOW!"

Yup. You guessed it. I had forgotten to tell Bobby that Mrs. Nelson's response to his live frog ending idea was a big "NO! Absolutely not!"

Joey, Rodney, Bobby, and I sprang into action. We chased after the frogs as fast as we could, down the hallway, past the securely closed door to the Principal's office, knocking things out of place as we went. The closer we got, the faster the frogs jumped as they headed for the exit door.

Just as the school janitor entered the building, Rodney lunged to tackle the closest frog, only to miss and slide across the hallway floor. Seeing the frogs in his path, Mr. Ellis opened the door wide, shooing the frogs down the school steps into the lush grass around the playground. He had aided and abetted their escape.

"Thanks, Mr. Ellis, but we got to go after them." We said in unison. Mr. Ellis' smile turned into a frown as his eyes took in the path of destruction. Every trash can lay on the ground, and Mr. Ellis's once shiny waxed floor was covered in wet frog footprints dotted with scuff marks from our shoes. "You boys need to turn around and go back to your room now."

Slinking our way back to the classroom, Joey anxiously whispered, "Freddo. Do you think we'll get fired by Miss Williams?"

I had no idea, but I was pretty sure that if she could, she would.

Chapter Nine
I'd Like to Play a "Do-Over" Card Please

I don't have any recollection of the
rest of the school day. On the way home,
Joey and I bought as much penny candy
as we could afford and ate it all before
supper. It didn't help.

The next morning, my puppet team
quietly slunk into our assigned seats. The stage was gone.
The table stood upright against the wall, supporting piles of
mimeographed papers, books, and other seatwork.

Mrs. Nelson did not look at us directly. No matter. The real
punishment came from the looks we got from all the girls. Each
one knew that any of their plays would have done much better,
and none of them would have caused Miss Williams to flee the
classroom for her life.

To make matters worse, Bobby was still sulking over the
loss of his pet frog Jumpy. With Bobby's frogs all missing, and
all that had happened, I felt pretty miserable. This had to be the
worst day in my seven years at Cleveland Avenue Elementary
School. At least Wendy was happy to get her tiger puppet back,
mostly unharmed except where the tape had pulled off some
fur.

Just as the lunch recess started, Mrs. Nelson pulled my team
aside. "Boys, I hope you learned a lesson from all this."

Not daring to say anything in reply, we all listened with downcast eyes.

Mrs. Nelson continued to say that everyone must learn from their failures so they can do better in life. She advised that in the future, we needed to go over all the steps of a project in our minds, taking time to think about what could go wrong, and then planning steps to avoid them.

Finally, she said the most important thing was to "Practice, practice, practice."

After the lecture was done, she looked at each of us, one at a time as she spoke, starting with Joey. "If you promise me that you will make all the changes you need and practice, practice, practice, we will invite Miss Williams back, and your team can try again."

Like an out of tune church choir, we responded in a jumble of voices, "Yes, Mrs. Nelson. We will. Yes, ma'am. Uh-huh. Really. REALLY we will!" To my surprise, Rodney didn't yawn the entire time.

Well, we took that second chance. Thinking through all of what had happened, my team practiced the play three times after school. Under the watchful eye of Mrs. Nelson, we were ready.

This time, it went without a hitch. The newly decorated throne room had a coat of arms on the wall bearing the image of frogs with ball tipped crossed sticks, more resembling high-tech fly swatters dipped in silver paint than anything else.

A green and yellow flag with its pole stuck in a spool of green thread sat next to a new paper fern tree, and a bigger, stickier gemstone was ready in the treasure box.

My team personally built the stage floor out of cardboard, thumbtacking it to the bottom side of the wooden tabletop. My dad gave me a new kind of space-age glue to make sure the strings stuck to the rocket.

Rodney's idea to use clear plastic film across the entire path of the cardboard rocket flyby to prevent any hang-ups at the window frame edges was pure genius.

There were four mimeograph copies of the script at school, and two copies at each of the boy's homes, for a total of twelve scripts that all showed up on the day of the do-over performance.

Finally, we made Bobby swear, "Cross his heart and hope to die" that he would not bring any frogs to school.

On the day of the play, all the right puppets came to school, and this time, Miss Williams sat in a comfortable chair in the first row three feet away from the stage.

Just before the performance, Mrs. Nelson told my team just how proud she was of us for not being afraid to try again. We beamed with bright smiles from ear to ear. We were in Mrs. Nelson's good graces once more.

As the curtain rose and rocket noises filled the classroom,

we caught a glimpse of Mrs. Nelson at the back of the room. Her face lit up with a confident smile, assuring us that we could do it right this time.

Looking down at Captain Carson, hiding in position as the *U.S.S. Destiny 1* rocket eased to a soft landing, a perceptible wave of confidence swept over me. I had said my prayers that morning, and I'm pretty sure Joey, Bobby, and Rodney did too.

No gaping holes appeared on the stage floor, and the throne room's departing rocket flight made it past the window frame without a snag.

At the end of the play, the entire class, teacher, and principal were standing and clapping. As for the four boys of Team 5, Joey took a deep bow, Rodney and Bobby shook hands and laughed, and as for me, well, I just looked out at all the girls and grinned.

The End

Fredd's Fractured Glossary
of Interesting Facts

Baseball Card Noisemaker - With a clothespin holding a favorite rookie of the year baseball card to your bike frame, you could make a great *'thwack-thwack-thwack'* noise as the bicycle spokes went whizzing by. More often than not, a kid trying to be cool never considers collecting baseball cards as a long term investment. If I had just kept one prized baseball player card in my sock drawer, I could pay for my grandkids' college tuition costs, books included.

Bell X-1 - The first aircraft to break the sound barrier. It was designed and built by Bell Aircraft, which is where my dad worked in Niagara Falls, N.Y. The pilot, Captain Chuck Yeager, had the name "Glamourous Glennis" painted under his cockpit window in honor of his wife, Glennis. Back then, flying planes, especially rocket planes, was a dangerous business, so all pilots got the OK to paint anything they wanted on the aircraft fuselage.

Bookmobile - A truck turned into a library on wheels by mechanically talented librarians. The bookmobile only had one aisle with books on both walls so that nobody could get lost looking for *Alice in Wonderland*.

Captain Midnight - Captain Jim was the star of the *Captain Midnight* TV show. He got his nickname, Captain Midnight, from an Air Force General after the Captain returned from his first dangerous mission precisely at midnight. Captain

Midnight flew a <u>Bell X-1</u> looking plane around the world to foil plots against the United States, sometimes taking only a few seconds to fly to the South Pole and back.

Curb Feelers - My mom loved driving, but a lot of times, she'd get too close to the concrete curbing and would scrape up the white-wall tires. To solve this problem, Dad installed a pair of curb feelers that looked like 10 inch long springs with a metal tip to do the scraping instead of the tires. Whenever Mom drove too close to the edges of the street, the curb feelers would make a loud screeching sound, which was a lot better than hearing Dad yell, "Marie! Watch the curb!" Come to think of it, Dad still said that a lot.

DEFCON 1 - All moms come equipped with a built-in DEFCON warning system, which is short for *D*etect *E*ngage and *F*reak-out *Con*dition status level. The national alert system used by the United States military, **De**fense **Con**dition (DEFCON) is designed the same way. For moms and the military, a DEFCON 5 status means no worries, life's great, be happy. At DEFCON 1, you can bet there's going to be big trouble if you don't act fast. Loud yelling and panic are allowed at this alert level.

Dewey Decimal System - To find a book in the library or bookmobile, you had to go to a card file, open a drawer, and look for the book you wanted by author or title. After copying down the Dewey Decimal System number from the card, you started searching. If you found that number printed on one of the thousands of books in the library, you were a lucky duck. It was like a treasure hunt with one big clue. Kids could be found wandering around lost most of the time looking for the book they were searching for. Unless you were in a big hurry, it was kind of fun.

Dudley Do-Right - Dudley was a Royal Canadian Mounted Policeman character who rode a horse and always did the right thing no matter what. In cartoon shows, his horse always helped save Nell (Dudley's girlfriend) from Snidely Whiplash. If you were a Dudley Do-Right, well that just meant you were upstanding and an excellent all-around person all the time – with or without a horse.

Explorer 1 - On January 31, 1958, the United States answered the Russian *Sputnik 1* satellite achievement with its own satellite, *Explorer 1*. What was neat about *Explorer I* was that it carried a scientific instrument that measured cosmic rays, which everybody knows is the stuff that powered Buck Rogers' laser gun. *Sputnik 1* just beeped for 21 days before its flashlight batteries died. Flashlight batteries didn't last that long in the 1950s.

Fountain Pen - Before ballpoint pens, these devices ruled the ink-writing world. Fountain Pens had a reservoir built into the barrel of the pen, allowing you to fill it and write in any color. I think they were called fountain pens because they tended to dribble ink like a sputtering fountain all over your homework assignment and shirt.

Hannibal's Soldiers – Hannibal and his soldiers used elephants to cross the Alps on their way to conquer the Romans.

157

Someone saw the spectacle and started the first circus using elephants as the main attraction.

Laundry Chute – If you ever tripped over dirty laundry piling up inside your bedroom, you need one of these. Our house had several 2-foot square wooden doors on the hallway wall connected to a long metal chute leading to the basement. To disappear your laundry, you simply opened the door, tossed in dirty clothes, towels, and smelly socks, and off they went to be washed. For any number of reasons, other things, like Ronnie's right shoe (April Fools!), a bad report card, or a box of cookies, sometimes found their way to the basement through this time-saving wonder.

Li'l Abner – Every Sunday morning, I started my newspaper reading with Li'l Abner because it was the first comic strip in the funnies section of the paper. Besides the main character, Abner, there were tons of supporting personalities like Honest Abe, Sadie Hawkins, Senator S. Phogbound, and Joe Btfsplk. Except for Fearless Fosdick, they all lived in the mountain village of Dogpatch, USA. Written and drawn by Al Capp, it was certainly better to read most of the times than the front page news.

Mickey Mantle - Mickey Mantle played center field on my favorite team, the New York Yankees. I'd listen to as many ballgames on my rocket ship AM radio that I could, oftentimes under the bedcovers after lights out. Just like *Sputnik 1*, portable radio batteries back in the 1950s didn't last long either.

Mimeograph Machine – Before photocopy machines, teachers could make multiple copies of anything as long as they used a typewriter to cut a special cardboard stencil. As the teacher cranked and fed individual sheets of paper under the rotating ink drum at the same time, the machine forced ink onto the paper making blue ink copies one at a time. If you made a mistake and tried to fix it, all you got was an unrecognizable blotch. One freshly cut stencil could only make about 24 good copies. As a result, school systems limited class sizes to less than 25 to keep teachers from either quitting or losing their minds. To say the least, it was messy.

Mud (Your Name is Mud) – Even before Dr. Mudd unknowingly patched up John Wilkes Booth, President Lincoln's assassin, if you did something people didn't like, they would say, 'Now you did it. Your name is mud!' It was like having real mud all over your clothes. Nobody wanted anything to do with you to avoid getting dirty too.

Naugahyde - My dad told me once that the covering on his electronics toolbox came from the hide of cute little animals called Naugas. The animals were helpful because they could shed their skin, over and over again, with no ill effects. My dad was always full of great information.

Niagara Falls, New York - Niagara Falls is over 400 miles away from New York City, so you can't go back and forth by subway even though some people think they can. Also, the City of Niagara Falls New York, U.S.A. sits across from Niagara Falls, Ontario, Canada, separated by the American, Canadian ("Horseshoe"), and Bridal Veil Falls.

The action of *1 million* gallons of water per minute crashing down 180 feet to the river below produces a thunderous and deafening roar. Iroquois Indians called this phenomena 'niagara' meaning, "These #$!@$% thundering waters are so loud, I can't hear a word you're saying!"

Old Country - My parents and grandparents considered the United States much newer than their own homeland back in Europe. Since the planet was pretty much all formed at the same time, how Europe was known as the old country always confused me.

Pie in the sky – Wishful thinking. Pie-in-the-sky ideas are usually half-baked ideas that don't require anything but a good imagination.

Rock-paper-scissors – If you didn't have a coin to flip, this was the international standard for settling arguments on things like who went first (or last), who got the first swig out of a bottle of pop, or who would tell Mom or Dad. Rumor has it that Niel Armstrong and Buzz Aldrin played rock-paper-scissors to see who would step on the moon first.

S&H Green Stamps – It was fun licking and pasting all the stamps Mom and Dad collected at the checkout counters of local supermarkets and gas stations. Once all 1200 stamps were pasted in the little squares found in each book, you could turn them in for kitchen gadgets highlighted in the S&H Gift Catalog. In my opinion, since there were no toys shown in the catalog, S&H could have at least used a better-tasting glue to make licking the stamps more fun.

Schwinn Bicycle - I learned to ride a bicycle on a Schwinn. These bikes were rugged. One time I crashed right into a big oak tree 10 seconds after the training wheels came off, and it didn't so much as scratch the paint. Even though they only had one speed, they were better than other bikes, mainly because the spokes on Schwinn bikes were sturdier. This helped the rider make louder *'thwack-thwack-thwack'* noises than other bikes using the same baseball card for a noisemaker.

Snow on the TV Screen – It wasn't the kind of snow you could use to make snowballs even though it did look like there was a blizzard going on inside your TV set. Snow of this kind happened when the television wasn't getting a signal either because the broadcast day was over or because your mom was running the vacuum cleaner in the next room. Whatever the cause, the result was a screen full of randomly blinking black and white blotches covering the screen. No matter what the season, this kind of snow would leave you out in the cold. Radios never had this problem.

Sputnik 1 - It was the first man-made satellite sent into orbit by Russian scientists. This feat so rattled the U.S. Government, that kids in my class ended up with tons more homework and new textbooks to teach us how to launch our own rockets. Even though all *Sputnik 1* ever did was send out a beeping signal for 21 days, it did start the race to the moon. Since I loved rockets and watching races, it was sure OK with me.

Superboy - If you have a perfect first issue of the *Superboy* comic series by *DC Comics*, you might be rich! Superboy crashed landed on a farm owned by Jonathan and Martha Kent somewhere outside Smallville, Kansas. Apparently, just before the planet, Krypton exploded, Jor-L, packed his baby boy, Kal El (Superboy), into a tiny spaceship and sent him to Earth without any care and feeding instructions. Luckily, Mr. and Mrs. Kent adopted Kal-El and gave him the super cool name of Clark. Just like my parents did, the Kents hid Superboy's spaceship so nobody would ask any questions.

The Willies - If you ever got the "Creeps," then you know the "Willies" – they are like relatives in the same family but with different last names. In either case, it means you aren't scared out of your mind right now, just freaked that something will really scare the living daylights out of you at some time, you just don't know when.

TV Broadcast Day - Television (TV) reception required a roof antenna and a long flat wire running down to the back of your TV set. Television programs only ran from about 7 A.M. to 11 P.M. each day to give the camera crews a chance to sleep. The TV station announcer would say, "And this concludes our broadcast day," just before the "Star-Spangled Banner" began to play. The broadcast day started with a test pattern, usually consisting of several circles and the face of an Indian Chief with his full ceremonial headdress appearing right in the middle of the screen.

TV Antenna – As television sets became more affordable, everyone bought one and installed a funny looking contraption on their rooftop. The antennas looked like an aluminum clothesline and were strapped to the highest point on the house (usually the chimney) to help it capture any available TV signal that was in range, which, depending on the size of your antenna, was about 50 miles. In Niagara Falls, we had two stations; Channel 2 and Channel 4 during the 1950s and 60s. If the weather was just right, sometimes we could tune in Channel 11, which was broadcast from Canada.

Tyrol (Tyrolean) - Remember the Treaty of Versailles? After WWI, a bunch of world leaders decided there were just too many countries, so they divided Tyrol between Austria and Italy. At least the Italian Province of Tyrol got its own American style football team named the Bolzano Giants and won the European Superbowl in 2009. Until they win again, Go Bills!

Vacuum Tubes - Vacuum tubes look like weird light bulbs and come in all sizes and shapes. Vacuum tubes controlled the flow of electrons and were used in amplifiers for rock-and-roll bands. Because of the invention of transistors, no one sees them much anymore. Back in the 60s, I used three vacuum tubes to build my own oscillating-electron-ion-engine.

Whirlpool Rapids Bridge - It is located a mile down the Niagara River from "The Falls" above an angry white-water whirlpool. The bridge itself is over 100 years old, with an upper deck designed for trains and a lower deck for cars and pedestrians. Foot traffic isn't allowed anymore, probably because people asked for their money back after experiencing just how dangerous walking across the bridge really was.

Meet the Author

Frederick G. Fedri(zzi)

While most kids in the 1950s wanted to be firemen or policemen, Fred wanted to be a writer for *MAD Magazine*. If that lofty goal failed, his second option was to become an astronaut.

Born in Niagara Falls, baby Frederick Fedrizzi could trace his ancestry to a country in Europe once known as Tyrol. When the family dropped the "zzi" from the end of their last name, forming the tongue twister 'Fred Fedri,' it was no wonder Fred had so many nicknames.

Fred loves to tell stories and episodes of his life to anyone who will listen. Many stories of his early childhood paint a picture of a time when life wasn't so complicated, and analog technology reigned supreme.

During his freshman year at the State University of New York at Buffalo, Fred's English professor valiantly tried to convince him to change majors from Mechanical Engineering to English. Unswayed because of Fred's wish to design houses for the moon, Fred stayed the course, graduating the year the draft lottery became mandatory for military service.

Graduating as the top honor graduate from the UH-1 Helicopter Crew Chief class located in Ft. Rucker, Alabama, he returned to his unit and was promptly assigned as a tractor-trailer truck driver because of the souped-up standard transmission hot rod he drove in civilian life!

Hired in 1972 at Westinghouse as one of the first computer system analysts, Fred turned away from the world of computing to marry Pauline and started work as a project engineer in North Tonawanda, N.Y. With a knack for writing, Fred found himself producing several newsletters. His Engineering Society of Buffalo *Unsupported Column* articles featured many humorous tales relative to the world of engineering and technology.

His work as a Communications Manager provided a unique opportunity to speak and present at STEM career day activities and Earth Day events. His presentation, "Spaceship Earth Is Now Hiring in All Areas," can continue to be enjoyed by students and teachers by downloading the STEM presentation at https://www.fedrifamilystories.com .

Recently discovered 1959 photo showing the author performing with Captain Carson on the front steps of his family home in Niagara Falls, NY.

Made in the USA
Columbia, SC
15 November 2020

24656160R00096